# Falling for Water

# Francesca Cairns

ASHWOOD
PUBLISHING

ISBN-paperback: 978-1-7641254-1-3
ISBN-epub: 978-1-7641254-2-0

Published by Ashwood Publishing, Cradoc, Tasmania.
ashwoodpublishing.com.au
info@ashwoodpublishing.com.au



Swimming woman image: Nettie Hulme
Cover design: Nettie Hulme/Susan Young

A catalogue record for this work is available from the National Library of Australia.

The work of Ashwood Publishing is nurtured by the beautiful country of the Melukerdee people in the Huon Valley in southern Lutruwita / Tasmania. We acknowledge and pay respect to the traditional owners and continuing custodians of this place.

*For Nettie
for the wonder,
for the light, and the deep.*

# Book One

# Chapter 1

Survival pushed Kayla up towards the light. Her logical mind screamed danger even as her mouth opened, desperate to source life from the very water itself. She drew deep gulps of liquid breath, saturating every cell with relief as though oxygen really had surged into her starving lungs. But, as always, this was the moment she would break with the dreaming, break through the surface into the glittering light of day. For one precious extra moment Kayla held her body tight, holding onto that waterborne breath till, giddy with need, she was forced to gag on the dust-laden air of her waking world.

It had happened again, same as before yet different. In the way an oral history shifts with the intonation. As a shoreline is sculpted by the tide.

There was no going back, not now … not ever of her own free will. Whenever she felt that restless thirst, Kayla would dream again. Dream of this place rich with water, its scant earth a tattered lacework framing myriad ponds and lakes. As if somewhere in her cellular memory was a map revealed only when she surrendered to sleep, slipping into the hidden wonders of the subconscious.

Kayla lay a while watching through the window as the sun climbed into the sky, the sweat of day gathering in the folds of her body. Reluctant to be here, forced to waken to this harsh, hot reality only heightened the contrast between realms. If only she could stay in that place, never compelled to surface, nourished by that sodden breath drawn so tangibly into the very pores of her being.

This longing was not new. Nor was the dreaming. Many times, Kayla had questioned her mother as to why she had to live here, in the arid air she woke to every day. But never had she asked about the invisible being, the elusive sense that there was another presence hovering in the periphery of her watery dreams. Somehow, she knew that one day, when she was deep or strong or wild enough, she would know who this watcher was.

Last week her mother had told her of how, after hearing Kayla calling out in the night, she had come into Kayla's room to be asked by her still dreaming child, "If I'm asleep now, who am I when I'm awake?" Her mother had laughed as she told the story, but Kayla sensed that it had made her mother uncomfortable, uncertain how to answer. There was something about this that was very important. If only she knew what. All she could remember of that night was being tenderly and safely held in the slow rolling rhythm of ocean waters.

It wasn't like she had webbed feet. Or gills for that matter. Kayla had checked often and thoroughly, certain she would find the watermark signifying her as different, but she never did. Yet there must have been something she couldn't see but others could. Something that kept her apart, unable to find friends like other kids did.

Her dad joked that whenever he was heading outdoors, he would find not only Toby the family dog waiting with wagging tail at the door, but also little Kayla grinning up at him, backpack ready to go. If he tried to sneak out without her, she would howl with misery.

Kayla really didn't care about what clothes she wore, but her mum and dad did. For years she had just gone along with it. But lately, frustrated by the annoying limitations of dresses, and the rules that went with them, she had stood her ground. Battle weary, her parents finally allowed her the freedom of clothes that could be patched and repaired. It wasn't that she ever wanted to be a boy, or particularly a girl, for that matter. She simply could not understand who had made up these strange rules for either. Pete, being two years older, and a boy, never seemed to have to worry about such things.

Under the bed lay the long green canvas sleeve that held her fly rod. She reached for it, needing the touch of her Nan, her grandmother, her mother's mother. How she loved this woman who had from the earliest of days taken her into the bush, encouraging her to run free and fearless through untracked forest. Then off to the rivers, to the lakes and the beach, where she'd taught her the nature of fish till she could tell what tugged her line and bring it in.

Over and over, with shiny-eyed excitement, Nan had enticed Kayla to share the moods and ever-changing ways of water, plunging her little hand, and then her shivering little body, into everything from bubbling streams to still and silent pools. Immersing her in the language, power and energy of water, and its relationship with the world. Awakening her senses to the gift of water, not only when it had fallen and pooled upon the earth, but when it danced in the sky, or caressed her cheek as rain or mist, hail or sleet. Kayla became as at home in the water as she was on land, and could swim, dive and paddle with fearless competence.

Stories flowed from the older woman of her young life in a village in remote Newfoundland, set upon rocky cliffs, entirely dependent on fishing, and weather, and sheer determination.

Woven between were stranger tales of deep, dark places and creatures capable of spell making and other unworldly ways.

Sometimes, as her Nan spoke, Kayla would shiver as she recognised images from her own dreaming. Little things like the different way light played in the woods or the sparkle of sun through water. Other times, her Nan would tell of murky inhabited depths, affirming the sense in Kayla that behind everything, something or someone was there, waiting, watching …

Throughout the days whiled away together, Kayla felt an urgency in the telling. That Nan was afraid of losing something, and it was really important that Kayla help hold to the words and wisdoms of the older woman.

But a little girl forgets. Kayla was only nine years old when Nan died suddenly one night in her sleep and was gone from Kayla's world as completely as she had been present. All that was left was the unwritten lore she had passed to Kayla, the memory of her strong brown arms holding little Kayla close and safe, and traces of the smell of her and their days shared in the rough canvas cover of Nan's old fly rod.

As Kayla's mum found no joy in fishing, Nan had requested that her fishing kit be passed on to Kayla, and so it was done. It had been her grandma's most cherished treasure, given as a gift from her parents when she married an Australian and moved half a world away. Kayla's great-grandfather had made the rod himself, her great-grandmother making the protective sleeve, embroidering the cover, stitch by loving stitch. Kayla's fingers lingered on the hand-sewn words she knew by heart: *With Love Always, Piccarie, Long Island, Newfoundland.* Now dulled with age, the fine threads still held strong, an indelible Braille-like message Kayla could reach for day or night.

Images flittered through her mind of houses and a village,

of cliffs and wild seas, created from stories and memories not her own. Asked when they could go there, her Nan used to get that faraway look. "One day, maid," she'd say in the speak of old Newfoundland. And then she'd smile at her in that way that was all mystery and magic and mischief rolled up together, and they'd laugh as though sharing a secret promise. "One day, maid," Kayla whispered to herself.

Kayla had been raised in the sprawling city of Melbourne. Summers were hot and long and kids here swam as easily as they walked. Summers began with a good scorching, the burnt, tender skin relieved at night with slices of cool tomato or cold teabags. She remembered the strange fascination of peeling off the thin membrane of blistered skin in as large as piece as possible. From then on, the fire of the sun was never given another thought, a dark tan worn like a badge of beauty and sun-worthiness in a land that worshipped blue-sky days.

Years ago, in a show of teaching Kayla to swim, an uncle from her dad's side of the family had taken her into the swirling waters of Half Moon Bay and let her go. Kayla would never forget the fear as she went under, then finding the trust, just as her Nan had taught her. *Always remember, child, that you are this water, and this water is you.* Without a splash, Kayla had glided away just under the surface, leaving him floundering with panic at her disappearance. Little did he understand that this was her medium, her air, her dreaming, and it held her buoyant and safe.

Kayla swam whenever and wherever she could, sometimes at the beach, mostly down at the nearby disused quarry or, when there was no other choice, at the local pool. Though she loved the ocean, the sand and the dynamic fun of the surf, there was often a disquieting moment when she would wonder if this was the day she would lose all that which held her separate from the salty blue water and simply disappear. In complete contrast, the pool was where she had to keep her skin zipped up tight, impermeable to the strange flavour of the bright clean water. But the rivers were always her favourite, where she could swim without fear of intrusion or dissolution. Rivers were happy, gurgling places, always coming from somewhere and going someplace else.

Then there was the local quarry. Here she often surfaced feeling strong and secure, almost triumphant. Kayla heard that some twenty years earlier, on an ordinary day of blasting and hauling stone, the quarry workers had broken through into the age-old tunnelling of an underground stream. Releasing the pressure of aeons, water had burst upwards, forcing the workers to retreat. By the time they returned next morning any machinery left on the quarry floor was mostly irretrievable, and within a week the quarry was more than half-filled and never worked again.

Holding her breath longer than any other kids, Kayla would disappear into the dark waters, returning with remnants of the old workings. Pieces of plunder she treasured in the way children value the revealing of things hidden and aged. Items possessed by a past to those who would listen, like the magic of the song of the sea in a shell.

There under the water, built into the slope of the quarry, she found the barely clad skeleton of an old hut. Loose tin swayed with the movement of the water, the doorway a gaping black hole of mystery. Her third dive saw her glide across the threshold into what would become her chamber. Kayla never told anyone about the hut where she would sit till her lungs were screaming, her mind on the brink of unconsciousness, willing herself to step from awake into dreaming. To trust the watery breath.

Yet always life's love for itself would drive her back to the surface to gasp on the arid air of the Australian summertime. Afterwards, disconsolate and chilled to the bone, Kayla would lie on the hot rocks and stare into the burning blue sky until the shivering melted from her body.

Between these decaying sheets of rusting iron, limited only by oxygen deprivation, Kayla had created a world all her own. She scrounged old biscuit tins and filled them with pencils and special leaves and feathers, weighting them down with her favourite rocks. Old crockery and cutlery added to the fantasy.

One day Kayla set up a lifeline to the world of air above with a length of worn garden hose, and nearly drowned when it slipped through the noose of her own making and into the water just as she was taking a triumphant breath below. Kayla was still not quite sure how she made it back to the surface. She trained day after day to extend her lung capacity, to eke out the used breath slower and slower, but little changed. Gradually she admitted she would always have to return to the stark reality above, to the isolation of a drop separated from the ocean, with the same inherent longing to return to the source.

But the old hut was only ever a short-term solution, an illusion of sanctuary. Swinging by the quarry in the midst of a drought-stricken summer, Kayla found a gang of men erecting barbed-wire-topped chain-link fencing. Large tankers and pumps sat on trailers, queued to drain the quarry of the water needed to save the surrounding parklands.

She returned a few days later just as the falling waterline dissolved around the loose tin and hardwood skeleton of the old shed. How different it looked in daylight! Weakened sheets of rusted iron collapsed down through the framework as the water continued to drop, till all that was left of her haven was a ragged collection of tortured metal, and a few stubborn sentinels of tired, waterlogged timber.

Kayla stood the rest of the afternoon in the shadows of the tall gums on the periphery. So many memories. It was hard not to grieve the loss, even as the thrill of adventure bubbled up through her body as it always had, irrepressible and intoxicating. She had been so young and brave and determined all at once. It really was impressive. And wonderfully foolish. How her Nan would have loved this secret world.

Then suddenly, it was as if Nan was right there, encouraging, emboldening her to step through her fears. It was time to go. The strength and courage she had found beneath these waters would never leave. But there was a liberty in this eviction that would force her to move outward and beyond. Within the walls of this old quarry, she had been dammed like a salmon separated from its ocean home. Out there somewhere was her river to the sea.

# Chapter 2

When Kayla was ten, her mum drove her and her brother Pete to stay with their father's great-uncle Ed on his soldier settlement holding in the Mallee, a hundred acres of scrub and sand. Kayla heard her mum say she couldn't imagine why anyone would want to stay in such barren land, but by the end of the first day neither child wanted to leave. Ever.

Located on the fringe of the great red inland desert, the Mallee was country of scarcity, with rare seasonal rains. The key was water. Always water, mostly too little, occasionally too much. Then every now and again there would be a year of exquisite balance, when the farmers would secure full ripe crops and pay off debts, squirrelling away any extra for the next hard years that would surely come. But it was a fragile landscape, violently cleared with giant rollers and chains. These monster machines had ripped out the tenacious roots of generations of scrubby woodlands, dense clumps of grasses and gnarly drought-hardened trees. Innumerable populations of rabbits had compounded the deforestation.

Ed showed them how, years back, he had located an unexpected stretch of damp ground. Slowly and with great patience he unearthed an underground spring, which now seeped steadily into a small wetland he had fenced and planted. Local shrubs and small trees had emerged, providing groundcover and sanctuary for an orchestra of grateful birds. Sheep manure and trace elements had enriched the adjacent sandy loam paddock. Over time the short but valuable annual harvest of an eighth of an acre of asparagus became enough to help cover Ed's land taxes and a few weeks break in Mildura, and keep his ageing Holden ute on the road. Along with a clutch of feral chickens roosting in the overhanging peppercorn trees, Ed ran a small flock of sheep. Several acres of primroses and a small crop of oats were cultivated for their grazing. "I am a man well contented with a solitary life, away from the madness and sadness of the world," he would often repeat.

Never one to hold back an experience, Ed roused the two kids out before dawn. Morning began with tea and toast, followed by a slow crawl in the breaking light along Ed's network of rabbit traps, whose catch paid for the basic supplies of a simple life. Within days they had learnt to set a rabbit trap without bloodying their own fingers, and to handle knives and death. Soon they were both adept with all aspects of the trapping, skinning, gutting and pairing of the captured rabbits, as the morning's bag was prepared for town. Out on remote tracks, he taught them the basics of driving the old Land Rover. He would walk the trap line while one or the other hopped and jumped the old farm truck along behind him. By the end of the first week they had both learnt to master the stiff clutch and gears.

They helped yard the flock of sheep, learning the difference between lamb, two-tooth, mutton and breeders, and the sadly destined wethers, those young males castrated for future eating. After cutting out a young wether from the flock, Kayla and Pete watched every detail of the slaughter and skinning till the strangely naked carcass was ready to hang to age and tenderise for the table.

The basics of throwing a return boomerang and splitting wood were promised in the week to come. Kayla couldn't get enough of this simple provisioning of one's own life. Never one for the mundane domestic chores at home, for the first time since her Nan died she felt the warm thrill of participation in tasks that mattered, part of something beyond herself and old as time.

Kayla and Pete poked their noses into every fascinating nook and cranny of Ed's realm. Old implements and tools, countless boxes and tins spilled out of numerous slab sheds with fruit crate shelves. Ed didn't mind what they opened so long as they didn't move stuff about. Despite the apparent chaos, he actually had a pretty good idea where to put his hand on anything he needed.

Ed had pointed out the prevalence of red-back spiders in the sheds and the trapdoor spider holes all across the yard. "As long as you shake out your boots and look before sticking your hand in anywhere, you should be right," he reckoned. "Oh and best to be watching out for snakes when you're poking under stuff, specially that old tin," he added after some thought.

Kayla found a pair of matching bent sticks tucked inside a shed door. They were nothing really, but she couldn't leave them alone. Pete had barely given them a glance as he disappeared through another doorway, framed with dusty spider webs.

Unable to resist, Kayla took one stick firmly in each hand. As she turned slowly in the circle of motley light, the sticks began to quiver. A tremor of fear passed through her, but not nearly strong enough to overwhelm the sense of magic, of power and knowing that became hers the moment her hands tightened around the worn wood.

Kayla followed the quivering tips out into the sunlight. The sudden glare was blinding, but she couldn't stop till she was standing beside the sheep trough, where Ed had been working since breakfast on a stubborn old pump.

Kayla never forgot the light of unexpected pleasure that shone from her Uncle Ed's eyes. "What you got there, girl?" he asked.

She shook her head with no idea how to reply. "Magic" the only word she could find.

"You'd be right about that," he said, reaching slowly across the gap and taking the rods gently from her hands. "Who'd ever have thought," he added, chuckling to himself. "So you got a bit of a feel for water then, lass?"

Kayla nodded solemnly.

"Let's you and me go for a walk." Ed took her hand and headed out past the woodheap into the next paddock burnt barren by a harsh white sun.

"Are they wands?" Kayla asked hopefully into the silence.

"You could say that," was all Ed offered. They came to the centre of the flat ground, the house and shady peppercorns now a smudge of hazy green on the horizon. Ed crouched down beside her. In the deep silence, Kayla wasn't sure if it was the leather of his old boots creaking or his long bones as well.

"These, my girl, are what's called dowsing rods. For those of us lucky, or maybe even special enough –" Here Ed stopped and gave Kayla a big wink. She was glad, and gave a tentative smile in return. It was all feeling a bit serious. "– special enough to have a feeling for it. These old sticks will lead you to water like you was following a bit of string."

"Water wands," she whispered.

Taking a moment to listen for her faint words, Ed nodded. "Yep, that's just what they are. Water wands." He passed them to her and watched as, without hesitation, she wrapped each little hand around the two ends, instinct bringing the long points upwards.

"Now I want you to shut your eyes." Kayla closed out the sharp glare of the sun. "Turn round slowly in a circle." She felt his hand on her shoulders, guiding her turn. "That's the way. Wait till you sense it." Ed's voice seemed to come from way outside. "You'll know when. Then open your eyes and follow the pull wherever it takes you."

Kayla turned as slowly as she could, till her feet were moving without thought, till there was nothing to know but the wands in her hands. She was starting to feel the strain of concentration when the sticks seemed to jerk slightly as if of their own mind. Time slowed as Kayla stopped, drew a long breath full of wishing, and moved the points back from where they'd come. There it was again, like a tug on a line.

Trembling slightly with the thrill that ran through her body, Kayla opened her eyes. One step after another, she set off across the dusty field. Under the shade of his hat, Ed crouched where he was, watching her advance unfailingly towards a distant star picket. Beaten firmly into the ground, it marked the meeting of two underground streams he'd been considering for a future bore.

Kayla sensed Ed come up beside her at the very moment the wands crossed. Looking up into his shining eyes, Kayla knew without being told that this was exactly what they were meant to do, that these quivering sticks had taken her straight to a stream that flowed deep underground. She stood longer, mesmerised by the strange sensation rippling through her body, as if filling her with something bigger than herself. She could feel Ed waiting, like a mountain, at her side, and felt no fear. After a time, not wanting to speak any words that might drain it away, Kayla silently offered the rods back to Ed. As if he knew just how much she didn't want to let them go, he indicated she might like to carry them home. She sure did! With her other hand she took his, and together they walked slowly back to the house.

Like a bottle uncorked, Ed poured out tales of dowsing, his own experiences and many he had only heard of, mostly successful, some downright dry and disappointing. It was the first time since losing her Nan that Kayla had felt seen for that which made her different, that held her apart, and she soaked it up.

Over the next few years, Kayla headed to the Mallee every given chance, apprenticing herself to Ed's side as he travelled here and there, following the calling for fresh water so integral in the Australian story of survival. Kayla could point at water with unerring certainty. Ed encouraged her to find her own special wands. Though she learned that her intent was more vital than the choice of rods, those first bent sticks were to become the treasure of a lifetime.

# Chapter 3

As her fourteenth birthday approached, Kayla felt increasingly isolated from her family and peers, this otherworldly awareness, untrained and maverick that it was, constantly at odds with the world she inhabited. And as for the under-stimulating, slow-moving school curriculum – it was enough to anaesthetise any inquiring mind into catatonic submission.

She began to withdraw, disappearing into a scatter of haunts she'd discovered in pockets of remnant bush left standing along the local creek. Anytime she could slip the noose she was gone, weekends or school days, it didn't matter. With her bathers, pillow, books and lunch, she could while away hours drifting and dozing to the gentle harmonies of life flowing by.

With adolescence came a new kind of dreaming. Familiar images now intensified as Kayla's nights became restless, unsettled. Primal images of land and fire, of skins and furs, came and went with no thread or story to bind them. And water, always water everywhere, streaming, tumbling, and pounding on rocky shores. Roaring tides dragged sea-rounded stones back into cold oceans, tossing them over and over with each crashing wave. Kayla had never known such sea or heard anything so powerful, yet there was something familiar and deeply comforting in its rhythm.

It was an ordinary winter's night, when Kayla was tucked up at home in her warm bed, that She first appeared. Kayla had always hoped, had imagined, that eventually someone or something would come or reach out or connect, that behind all the images and sounds of her dreaming was a presence that time would reveal.

Sleep had drawn Kayla into a shrouded world of murky green, gradually revealing a shadowy forest of lichen and spruce. This landscape she knew. Her dreaming had often begun in woods such as these before melting into images of vast lakes, of rock-strewn rivers and intimate hidden pools. But they were scenes she had only been able to look upon, or into, blurred and ill-defined as if through a rainswept window, with the hushed soundscape of the very deep. This night the sound gradually cleared till she could hear the gurgling conversation of a stream tumbling over stones and crevices, like a background murmur of adult voices interspersed with the bubbling exuberance of the young.

The creature came then, as if from and out of the landscape all at once. As if from the shadows and yet separate. A body formed, at first animal, then gradually more human. From within a hooded cowl eyes gleamed, then the face of a woman emerged, lined and weatherworn, soft and round and fresh, yet young and old all at once as if fluid with time. For a moment Kayla fell, lost in deep dark pools of ancient eyes. Without being told, Kayla understood that this was She who had always been there, part of her dreaming for as long as she could remember.

"Nunik," she whispered, somehow knowing this was the name she would use. Tenderness lit the woman's face, creasing her eyes, breaking the trance. Abruptly, she slid smoothly down the bank, disappearing beneath spreading ripples.

Without hesitation Kayla followed into water so shockingly cold it took her breath away, but there was no time for thought. Her muscles burned with the effort of keeping up with the flick of feet. Or was that a tail? Whatever it was, it was all she could see of this being who'd finally come. She took a dream breath and then another as she had practised all those years – salt! They must have left the stream for the ocean.

Kayla followed a trail of bubbles ever deeper into wondrous depths, weaving among fish and swaying sea gardens as naturally as though she had been born in this realm. Gradually everything merged, becoming one, and she woke alone, in her own bed. She lay for a while, still and silently ecstatic. For once her breath was gentle and slow as if she had simply moved from one way of breathing to another, then back again. All those years growing up, secretly wondering if she really was a mermaid or a seal or suchlike, no longer mattered.

It was months before she came again, this Nunik, but that didn't matter either. Her dreams, her Nan, and now her Nunik, shared a secret knowing. Something strengthened in Kayla. A bridge had formed, linking her separate realms, reawakening the awareness of mysterious wonder gifted from her Nan, found in the faintest lift of a drifting mist just as powerfully as in the electric thrill of a storm-charged sky. At last Kayla was not alone, and the beauty of dreams was that she could be anything she wanted …

# Chapter 4

School lost all its charm. Sometimes she went but mostly she didn't, and it was causing all sorts of problems. After barely scraping a pass to Year 9, Kayla agreed to try harder, but the February classes droned on and on. The sentence of three more years was just not worth thinking about.

Lately she'd taken to watching the evening news, fascinated and yet repulsed by the worsening revelations of each day. The world was becoming more frightened and frightening all at once. Headlines of wars and famines and ecological disasters wove through the routines that she woke to every day.

Kayla tried, but nobody wanted to talk about it. Nobody seemed to care. Not her teachers, her mum or dad, and especially the other kids. One hot morning when both her parents had left early for work and Pete for school, Kayla emptied the books from her bag and repacked for the bush. She was done here.

But she was still only fifteen, so, not wishing to distress her parents, she wrote a note.

*Can't waste any more time at school. Gone to Ed's. Will call soon. Don't worry. I'll be fine. Love Kayla.*

Then she screwed it up. Ed had no phone. She didn't want them driving up there.

*Dear Mum and Dad and Pete. I have decided to travel and work and learn from life what I can't get from school. I will call and let you know I am safe. I am sorry I know it's not what you wanted. Try not to worry, love Kayla.*

Then realising how much they would worry, added *PS I will be at Ed's and will give you a call.* There was no way to get it right, so she left it anyway.

Kayla caught a train to Albion Station where the Sunbury railway line crossed the highway to Ballarat. In all honesty, she was more than a little nervous as she stepped off the kerb to hitch a ride. Minutes later a small truck crammed with market produce pulled up just ahead of her. *St. Arnaud's Fruitier* was painted on the side door. This was perfect: St Arnaud was on the Sunraysia Highway and about halfway to Ed's. With a sigh of relief, she found room for her bag and rod in the back and hopped into the cab. It was going to be all right.

Kayla reassured the couple inside that she'd run out of money and was only hitching a ride to get home. It was a lie she found allayed concern, and it was sort of true. George and Stella, returning with a load of produce from the Footscray wholesale market, were happy to be on the road north. When they dropped her in front of the St. Arnaud town hall, Stella insisted Kayla accept a bag of fresh fruit and veg.

Two more rides via Donald and Lacelles and she made it to Hopetoun, the nearest town to Ed's place. Out the front of a local café she got chatting with two young mechanics who offered to drive her to Ed's farm even though it was out of their way. It was the scariest choice of the day, as they were out to impress with speed and bravado. It had just gone six in the evening when the car pulled up in a cloud of dust at the stand of gnarly eucalypts that marked the gateway into Ed's place.

Waving the mechanics off, Kayla turned to look up at the rambling old house she was so fond of. It wasn't much of a hill, but she still had more than the track to climb. It was time to convince Ed.

There were no dogs to alert him to her presence, yet she wasn't surprised when he met her at the door.

"Well, what have we got here, then?" he asked, swinging the screen door wide with welcome. With a cup of hot, strong tea came the questions. Ed was no pushover. They would be off to the neighbour's directly to call her parents. That was non-negotiable.

"Tell me why I ought let you stay, young Kayla?" he asked, pinning her attention with the seriousness of his tone.

Suddenly she did feel young, very young and small and maybe even foolish … naïve even. Well, maybe she was all those things, but she was more than that, stronger than he knew. Sometimes she even felt so old that the deepest part of herself was worn out with trying, and she wished she was just young and carefree. No matter how she tried, she never really felt that way. That there were things she had to do or make happen and she didn't even know what … that she couldn't just keep pretending she saw the world like the other kids cause she didn't … and anyway she'd been alone forever since her Nan died because no one else got that she had this other life that came at night with her dreaming and everything that ever meant anything to her ended up being about water … always about water …

It poured out in a torrent of words, spilling across the table and over this man, the only other person in the whole world who Kayla knew loved water as if it were blood, their blood, earth's blood, the most important thing of all. He had to hear her … He just had to …

For some minutes Ed said nothing, letting the crackle of the wood stove take the edge off the silence. "Why here, Kayla? What is it you think I can offer?"

"It's everything …" she began. "It's getting up in the morning before the sun. It's eating your own food you're responsible for. It's cooking with wood – hell, it's even getting the wood in the first place." Kayla stopped. Nothing of these things were it. "Actually, it's really just you, Uncle Ed. The way you live. The way you think. That you fill each day with things that matter and even that these things matter to you – the wind, the weather, the bush. And then there's the whole thing about water and dowsing … and you know other things … the stuff behind what most people see … I see it too."

She lifted her chin. Kayla knew she looked hard-headed, but held Ed's gaze till his face softened with the slightest of smiles. "I'll give you three months. That is if your parents can handle it. You'll do everything I ask … and you can ask me anything. Agreed?"

Three months later Kayla's mum and dad dropped by. They arrived unannounced, though not unexpected, and Kayla couldn't help but think they'd meant to catch her out somehow. Even as they were saying hello she peered past them, scanning the back seat for Pete, but he wasn't with them. It turned out he'd gone hiking in the Grampians. Her shoulders slumped. To her surprise, she really did miss him. Maybe she'd make the effort soon and give him a call.

Following a chatty dinner, her parents stayed the night, leaving in the early morning on their real holiday, a week on a houseboat up on the Murray River near Mildura. After waving them off in an overly cheery farewell, Ed and Kayla stood together by the house, watching the dust dwindle into the distance.

"Well, I guess that's that," Ed said.

"Suits me," Kayla muttered.

"So you're not missing them then?"

"About as much as they're missing me. I think it's easier this way."

"You might just be right about that." Ed lifted a hand and tousled her hair. "Suits me too, just so you know. Now how's about we empty that ute."

# Chapter 5

"Kayla … Kayla. Can you hear me? Kayla."

She could, but she didn't want to yet. She felt like a mountain on a grey misty day, her head and shoulders shrouded in thick clinging cloud. Vision blinded, voices muted, the air dense with moisture – and something else gritty with shards as sharp as shattered glass, tearing at her throat, dragging her deeper into the darkness. She was vaguely aware of her body as it thrashed about, of the spasm in her lungs as she struggled to draw breath. Someone turned her onto her side. A wave of nausea turned into retching and a clammy sweat that left her shivering in the hot afternoon sun.

"I'm OK," Kayla managed to mutter from somewhere still far, far away. The edge of anxiety in the hands that held her gradually relaxed into a gentle stroking motion, keeping her from slipping further back. Slowly the passage of her breathing eased, her body softening into the sandy bed.

Kayla emptied her mind of thought, seeking that calm centre of the storm. Movement swirled behind her closed eyes, a gentle dance of tiny, crystal-clear droplets swaying in a light breeze. Clean, sweet moisture. Her breathing deepened as she drew healing breaths into her bloodstream, pushing out the residual darkness. She opened her eyes and caught a fleeting glimpse of concern etched in the lines of Ed's big face as it hovered above hers. Then it was gone in the gawky grin of relief that took its place.

"Welcome back."

Kayla nodded, slowly sitting up. "Thanks."

She was glad the landowners had wandered off. Fresh from an urban life in Sydney, Brenda and Gary had bought this small farm south of Bathurst to raise alpacas, an animal still novel to Australian farmers. Ed and Kayla had made the ten-hour trip from home the previous day, hopeful they could help locate an underground source of water for the growing herd.

Kayla had known this weird feeling before, but never like this. Never had it swept her feet out from beneath her, dropping her to the ground like a stone. But neither had it had the clarity, the absolute certainty with which she could now say, "This water's no good, Ed."

Ed nodded, giving it the considered thought that was his way. "Figured that. How so?"

She'd been dreading this part. If only she could show him how she felt, have him feel the filth the way it swept over her.

"It's like the poison of it gets into my veins, into my blood. And I sort of feel the pain of it, only it's not my pain but the distortion in the water itself, as if it's trying to resist the damage, trying to rid itself of whatever's infected it. Today was cutting." Her body shivered as if trying to shrug away the thought. "Sharp and dark and filthy, worse than any other time. It's like ..." Kayla stopped, searching for words, reaching deeper. "It's like I can see, but not with my eyes, the shape or the state of it. Not of the drops themselves but inside it. Patterns and shadows like marks or moods of where it's been, of how it's been made. I know when it's right 'cause then it's kind of happy and flowing. Today it was like little torn sacks of broken glass repelling each other, hurting so much that it could hardly bear to be touched."

Ed nodded. "You'll be all right now?"

"Yeah, I'm good. But something's terribly wrong down there, Ed. I just know it. They'd be mad to drill here."

They both watched Brenda and Gary pottering around an old shed in the distance. "I guess I'll advise them against it," Ed said after a couple of minutes.

"Guess you better," Kayla agreed, surprised and moved by his unquestioned confidence in her perception.

A couple of months later, they heard through Ed's dowsing network that, after seeking a more favourable opinion, Brenda and Gary spent over ten thousand dollars before they reached water they could never use. Eventually the tailing dam of an old gold mine, located upstream, was found to be the culprit. Arsenic from the tainted mud had seeped through porous bedrock over the seventy years since it was abandoned.

She was glad she'd spoken up even though they hadn't listened. In the end the final result had confirmed her assessment. Even the disappointment and concern she felt for Brenda and Gary, the water table, and all the surrounding farms couldn't suppress the thrill of success. Time to do away with those old fears of ridicule, or a false reading. Finally, she had put words to this internal vision she had kept hidden, and it had proved to be true.

From then on Ed always took her with him, watched her for signs, listened to her concerns, and adapted his advice accordingly. Returning home late one evening, Kayla knew that Ed's unspoken confidence had changed something deep within her. And that she would remember this time, safe beneath the protective shadow of this humble Mallee farmer, as her first experience of strength found in the risk of trusting her own truth. Ed had once said to her, *You can't rely on the world out there to make up your mind. It only takes one person's trust to make all the difference, and sometimes that one has to be yourself.* He had shown her that day, by being the one.

# Chapter 6

They'd been a bit out of sorts for a couple of days. He thought it was her, but Kayla was certain it was him. Woken by the unusual sounds of Ed ferreting about his room, she was surprised to see him appear with a small case in hand. Just glad it wasn't hers.

"Time we got out of here for a few days, girl. Finish your brekky now and throw a few things in a bag. Reckon to be gone soon as we're fed and watered." Other than the fact that they had turned north, Kayla had no idea where they were going and didn't really care. It was good just to be on the road.

Ed was in no rush, never was for that matter, taking the road at no more than fifty miles an hour. "A mile's a good long distance," he'd say. "Kilometres is just a way to say you've done more when nothing's really changed at all, like a lot of things in this modern world."

Kayla kinda got the way he still thought in feet and inches. There was something timeless about him, just like these old roads where the occasional stumpy white mile marker could be seen peeking out of the roadside grasses, the next town's initials and the miles to go carved into its surface. They must have been made of redgum or stone to have lasted so long.

After a while Ed cleared his throat. "Taking you to Alice's place for a few days. I'm thinking you could do with the company of women." He glanced at her, gauging her response. Kayla tried for a smile, but it probably looked a bit weird.

"S'pose you'd be wondering who she is then?" Ed nodded, as if catching her thought. "Met Alice when I was driving stock trucks and been friends ever since. Must be near on thirty years ago. Saw a bit of them for a while, her and her husband, Nev. But she was always the one that carried the weight of that place. He's long gone now, and she'll be just the ticket, I'm thinking." He chuckled. "Don't worry, you'll like her, I'm sure. But not too much though. Remember that at week's end you're coming home with me."

That was reassuring. He wasn't sick of her then. "OK," Kayla agreed. She'd trusted him this far. No need to stop now. And yeah, a change of scene would be good.

Kayla leaned into the corner, lulled by the rhythm of the motor, the flicker of posts and telegraph poles straight and grey against the pale paddocks. She'd had some great chats on long drives like this. There was something about distances and spaces and the empty miles of travel that freed half-formed thoughts from the crevices of the mind. Maybe if she spoke now at least they wouldn't have to look at each other. It was definitely worth the risk. She took a deep breath.

"Ed?"

"Mm," then "Yes?" when she didn't go on.

"Do you ever wonder if water tries to tell us stuff, but we don't know how to listen?"

Kayla tried to watch him without turning her head, but Ed just kept his eyes on the road, so she did the same.

"What are you thinking?" he said at last.

"I don't know, I've been trying to find a way to describe it. I mean I know about minerals and rust and all the other stuff that makes water taste different … but this is not really about taste. It's like background or … mood or something … older." Kayla squirmed in her seat, concentrating on growing an idea she had never before put into words. "Well, you know how rain's sort of new and fresh, and storm drops have an electric tangy metal thing happening, and mists are soft and gentle like a warm hug, and fog … well, fog's like a wet, grey, soggy blanket …"

"Go on," Ed said into the ensuing silence.

Kayla took a deep breath, trying to draw the words from some-place beyond science and logic. "Sometimes when I've had a drink from a river, I can see where it's been as though a map forms in my head of all the ways the drops become trickles then trickles become streams like veins running into arteries, and I can taste – but it's not really taste – the excitement of bubbling over stones and it makes me laugh. Other times it's so deep and still all I can do is sit on the bank till it passes." Kayla sat a moment, quietened by the memory, the only sound the low growl of rubber on bitumen.

"Bores are weird though," Kayla continued after another glance at Ed. "I'd never had bore water before coming to yours. It's incredible how different each one tastes, but somehow the water always seems surprised. Like it's been woken up too soon and was shocked by the light."

"Yep. I get that," Ed said slowly.

Kayla liked the way he nodded as he spoke. He really was listening. "But springs are the best by far," Kayla continued. Just saying that made her grin. She really loved springs, especially when they gurgled out of the ground.

"It's like they've had all the time they need. And the water is so clean and full all at once. Only instead of a map it's a whole book, as though by seeping all the way down then coming up through the earth it not only knows the veins but also remembers the whole body it passes through. And you know when you drink it that it's the way it's meant to be." Kayla paused, searching for the right words. "Then there's something else about water from a spring being given, not taken."

"Fair point." Ed nodded again, slowly. "Well put."

Encouraged, Kayla ploughed on. "It all makes me wonder … whether water has a sort of memory. That each drop holds a kind of record of information that it brings to the whole, like a flock of birds, or a school of fish. The way they know all together, when and which way to turn. Maybe water can even remember what it needs to heal and recover, just like our bodies do when we get sick. What if, long ago when we roamed the earth, all wild and dependent on the elements, we could translate that stuff too? And so maybe there's a chance that one day we could remember what we used to know and work together."

More miles passed. "I knew a fella once who told me that water could tell him where it had been," Ed said finally. "Guess that's kinda what you mean?"

"Really?" Kayla asked, watching him now.

"Yep. He was sure of it. Said one day they'd be able to show it to be so. Said that one day we would learn to value the wisdom of water if we didn't taint it all first."

"Do you still know where he is?" Kayla couldn't contain the excitement in her voice.

"Sorry, love, but I imagine he has merged back into the rivers of time. Jimmy's been gone some twenty years. We used to ride the trains together, he and I. Best fella for knowing if water was good that I ever knew."

Kayla turned to the window, biting back emotion that burned her eyes. How could she miss something she didn't even know about till now? Her hands tightened into frustrated fists on her lap. She'd been born too late, the people she needed were dead. Except Ed, of course.

Ed gave her time before speaking. "There's no doubt that what you have here is a special kind of seeing, Kayla, knowing things beyond the rest of us, and I'll confess I'm a bit envious. And anyway, it seems to me you already have the answer to your question."

"What question? What do you mean?"

"The 'Where do I go from here?' Or 'What do I do with my life?' kind of question." Ed stopped as if still forming his words. Curious, Kayla waited him out.

"Be that translator, Kayla. Be the bridge between us and the things we've forgotten. God knows someone needs to. You're still young, and I know, no one likes to be told, but if you're listening, lessons come in the most unlikely of ways. I hold no fear for the teachings of nature. It's the foolishness of men that brings grief. And I tell you, girl, being a step on your path has made my life a damn sight more interesting." Then he laughed at his unexpected exposure. "Just listen to me then. You've got me rabbiting on just like you." But the look he gave her was soft, shy and tender, protective and proud all at once, and it lifted her heart.

# Chapter 7

Kayla's time with Alice was the balm she hadn't realised she needed. The kitchen she entered was bright and busy, the table a place of welcome and sharing in the way women do so well. Autumn produce lay spread out across the benches in various stages of preservation. Any thoughts of a restful time were dispelled after the first cup of tea, when paring knives and a bundle of fresh green beans were tabled ready to string, chop and prepare for blanching.

Located just out of the town of Patchewollock, Alice lived on a small block of a larger holding taken up after the First World War. Although over six hundred acres, it was arid and had never been fertile enough to support a large family using traditional farming methods. Some years ago, after four impoverished generations, Alice had sold off all but twenty-three acres to neighbouring farms.

"Suits me down to the ground now," Alice told Kayla as the beans flew through her practised hands. "For nearly thirty years I went off to work in town, but once Nev and the kids were gone I realised that I was only working to support a working lifestyle. It was the best choice I ever made. The order of the day is my own. There were a few lean years, believe me, but now I grow most of my own food and swap the extra for what I don't. I do bookkeeping from home and it's enough to keep the electricity and rates paid and the car on the road."

Alice kept talking even as she whisked the prepared beans into the pot, brought them to a rapid boil then plunged them into a tub of water and ice, halting the cooking instantly. The beans glistened green, ripe with life and tending. Kayla let the words roll over her, listening and nodding into the rare spaces. It was like rubbing oil into dry skin and by end of day she felt plumped, buoyant with an abundance of vibrant conversation.

The next morning, Kayla lingered longer than she intended in the soft bed. After barely a knock Alice bustled through the door bearing a tray laden with pancakes, homemade butter and jams. It was the sort of breakfast Kayla had only dreamt about lately. Mornings at Ed's began by the light of a kero lamp, a ritual of slow-brewed tea and bread toasted by the flames of the ancient Wellstood stove. Kayla loved those mornings, had learnt to savour every bite, curbing her hunger till she could fill up on the inevitable roasted lamb and damper for lunch. Alice set Kayla up with the tray and plopped down on the bed. Kayla managed only a few short replies as she worked her way to the bottom of the plate, but it didn't matter; Alice made up for both as she outlined plans for the day.

It was barely after nine when the first of a stream of women popped her head in through the front door. Some came bearing nourishment for the table, others with nothing but willing hands. But each came with a story or two of ordinary lives trying to find a way through, and each was given a chance to be heard. Some brought laughter, others tears. But that day, in that bustling, warm kitchen, Kayla became aware that for the first time that she had become one in a company of women. Barely fifteen when she had gone to Ed's, now, only nine months on, Kayla felt so much older, able to join in the conversation with surprising ease. Soon she was breathless with laughter, loving the wicked and mischievous humour women find in the safety of each other.

Each visitor required a cuppa and conversation, but the extra help made up for any time lost. Kayla had heard the saying "many hands make light work", but had never been a part of something so natural and organic in process, that seemed to have no leader or direction, just a continuous flow towards completion. And to take her part at such a table was as natural as breathing. Perhaps she wasn't so strange after all.

Over the next few years, Kayla spent precious time with Alice every few months. Although deeply nourishing, it was always busy and hectic, and she was more than ready to retreat to the quiet of Ed's when her week was up.

It was in the second year that she met Beth. Kayla noticed the strange car as she returned to the house with an armful of freshly picked corn. Struggling with her usual shyness she stopped on the steps for a deep, reassuring breath before pushing the screen door open. Suddenly there were hands reaching out to ease her load and she looked up into a face younger, and a grin cheekier, than any she had seen for a while, and there was nothing she could do but return the smile.

"Better give me some of that then," the stranger said as she took the weight, and together they lifted the load onto the bench.

"Thanks," said Kayla, wiping her hands on her pants as Alice bustled in beside her and placed a reassuring hand on her shoulder.

"Kayla, this is one of my nearest and dearest friends, Carol, and her niece, Beth. They'll be staying with us for the next few days."

Then, as if saving her from a response, the moment dissolved into a flurry of busyness as Alice directed each into their task in the preparation of the day's corn relish.

As was her way, Kayla watched, intrigued by the feisty conversations played out between Beth and her auntie. Beth seemed to challenge every other statement Carol made. Not so much as a naughty child might, obstinate and bloody-minded, but with relentless questioning as if Beth's mind was compelled to tease at any threads that given enough unravelling, might simply come apart. Rather than react, Carol seemed to encourage the exchange, sometimes agreeing to disagree, other times surrendering with a shake of head that spoke of an uncommon mixture of pride and defeat. Kayla couldn't help the taste of envy that arose. How she longed for such a relationship with a woman of her own kin.

Finally, looking for a moment's peace, Alice and Carol banished Beth from the house, sending her out for a dose of fresh air. From the door, Beth raised her eyebrows in an invitation Kayla couldn't refuse. They spent the rest of the day roaming aimlessly across paddocks, slipping between strands of wire when there were no gates, till they lost sight of the house. Beth had a commentary on everything, and Kayla was quite happy just listening, soaking up the youthful spirit of rebellion as it washed over her. She hadn't realised how old and serious she'd become.

"So what do you think?"

"What? Sorry I …" Kayla started, lost in her own thoughts. It was the first time Beth seemed to have stopped to draw breath since they left. "Think about what?"

Beth laughed. "Everything and nothing. This amazing planet we find ourselves on, circling a sun that could explode any minute. The self-importance we're raised to, as if we're something more than a heartbeat in a march of time that marks its passage in millennia rather than days and hours. Being part of a society that thinks it's OK to bomb defenceless civilians, to ravage, deplete and poison the earth, without thought of consequences and the future of the yet unborn." Beth stopped and grinned. "Just that sort of stuff."

Are you kidding? She had a library of ponderings about just these kinds of thoughts. At last someone her own age who actually cared. She loved Alice and had come to care deeply for many of the women who came to share, but they were so much older and many already set in their thinking.

On the bank of a half-filled dam, they found a patch of grass still green under the protective canopy of a stand of old gums. Side by side they lay back in the mottled light, rummaging through concepts from books they'd read, ideas they'd formed, dissecting and deconstructing, sharing as much laughter as righteous rage. Suddenly touched by the deepening colour of the setting sun, they had to run to beat the dark.

Heart racing, Kayla lay in bed that night unable to sleep. How was she so excited about this person whose world was so different, whose life was so far away, in the heart of the city no less? Even after talking and walking all day she hardly knew her, yet they seem to have become friends. Instantly. Conceived in the intangible realms of ideals and ideas, this connection had grown from that part of her that included more than the simple routines of daily life. Kayla snuggled deeper into her blankets, wanting to keep the warmth of the day, of the bonding, forever close.

As Beth and her aunt left the next day, Beth had passed Kayla her address, along with a tight hug. "If you're ever up our way, make sure you drop in." Kayla put it safely away.

It was a rare quiet moment, just the two of them sharing a cuppa as they waited for Ed to come and take Kayla home, when Alice said, "Now Kayla, before you go this time, we want you to know that there's not a woman among us who hasn't commented on the pleasure it's been to have you in our midst. You've grown from a girl into a fine young woman. What are you now? Seventeen? You may not realise it, but it's taken a certain courage to do what you've done."

A blush spread across her face even before she looked up into Alice's eyes, creased, as they were, with a smile echoing the genuine affection in her voice. Unexpected emotion choked any quick reply. Except for her Nan, and now Ed, no one had seemed to care terribly much whether she came or went. Her family loved her, of course, in their own family way. She knew that; they were supposed to. But she also knew that she wasn't quite like them and couldn't imagine ever settling for "life on the wheel", as Ed would say. But these women had taken her in, nurtured her without judgement, and she was so grateful.

Alice topped up both their cups before speaking. "There's a part in all of us that needs reminding that we make choices every day about the destiny of our own lives. It's all too easy, especially as you get older and more complacent, and less brave perhaps, to feel trapped in a direction you never really did mean to choose. God knows we've all done it." Alice shook her head as if dislodging a memory. "Now, Kayla, you know that Ed's family to us, not blood, but near as good as. So, this question comes with a great deal of respect for you both. As one woman to another, are you really OK out there?"

"You mean at Ed's? Yeah, it's great."

Alice didn't say anything, waiting, the question still alive in the tilt of her head. She clearly wanted more, but Kayla wasn't sure what to say. As she and Ed had travelled through the back lands dowsing and bartering for stock and various farming needs, other people had skirted around the same question, implying she must be lonely or possibly at risk. She was neither. But it was a caring question and deserved a real answer.

"I know why you're asking, but don't worry. Ed's cool. I haven't felt this safe since I was a kid." There it was. Kayla hadn't put it so clearly before, but it was true. Ed was a giver not a taker, and his gentle honour would never cross those boundaries. "Both of you have taught me so many things, and not just practical stuff. Things like about who I want to be, choices about how I want to live, and what I want to value. Ed's shown me how to be content with whatever way things turn out, in a way that I didn't know people could. 'So much ballyhoo about nothing', he says, and it's true."

"But what about friends? Don't you miss being with young people?"

That was easier. "Not really and yeah, sometimes. Sometimes I imagine what it might be like to have a best friend, but it never did happen so it's not like I miss anyone in particular. Mostly I don't think about it. I'm happy on my own, or doing something with Ed, or being here at your table tailing beans. Ed says 'You have to learn to live with yourself before you're any good to anybody else.' So I'm working on it." Kayla tried for a reassuring grin but wasn't too sure how it went. It was true, sort of.

Alice took her hand. "You are a dear soul, Kayla. I can't pretend to understand where your knowing springs from, but I am grateful to be a part of it. There's no doubt your life's journey will be far greater than anything you can yet imagine. But come what may, there'll always be a place for you here. Anytime. Any condition.

Curious little button you are, we've become rather fond of having you around."

Alice pulled her into a warm embrace, the kind of hug that wove strong arms into a safe cocoon. Fighting back, Kayla tried to push away but Alice held her close. A strange sound came unbidden, an unexpected mixture of grief and joy. Tears escaped, tears she didn't know she had, for things she had refused to admit she missed. Eventually she surrendered into the dark haven of Alice's soft body.

Alice held her till she was done, till Kayla rested to the steady reassuring beat of Alice's heart. Nothing had changed, yet as she pulled away, Kayla felt lighter, eased somehow by this close, nourishing warmth of another human being. Despite her want to be fiercely independent, she needed it just as much as anyone.

*Anytime, and in any way we can be there.* Alice's words followed Kayla as she slipped outside.

# Chapter 8

Kayla hoisted the tub of snap-fresh asparagus onto her shoulder, savouring the weight, the effort, and the sweat. It was only a short walk to where she'd parked the ute. After nearly three hours of harvesting there was still strength in her stride that made her just want to dance. This was the last tub to complete the load for town and it had only just gone 10 a.m. What a harvest it was.

Over the years, Ed and Kayla had mulched and manured and expanded the asparagus field with anything they could lay hands on. Now they were reaping the rewards. The rain had come at the right time and the shoots were thick and abundant.

Before jumping in behind the wheel, Kayla grabbed her water bottle and slipped easily over the wire fence, making her way to the small soak of clear water at the heart of the wetland. There in the moist green centre she sipped on the sweet, cool water, ripe and brimming with the nutrients gleaned as it seeped and flowed into and from the earth. It was one of Ed's primary teachings. *Take a moment in between to appreciate where you've just been.* She smiled, remembering how there'd been a few times when Ed had grabbed her by the collar to hold her that extra minute before she bolted headlong, and headstrong, into the next act.

And he was so right. Even with a capacity load picked and set to go, there was a satisfying green tinge right across the beds as tomorrow's harvest pushed into the light. Beyond the spring and its bounty, the surrounding paddocks were already heat-hazy with the coming day. Outside the fence line, dark smudges marked remnants of stunted mallee scrub, the only contrast between here and the distant horizon. Big land. Vast distances, bereft of humans, yet indelibly changed by their presence.

Kayla rubbed her shoulder where the tub had rested. It was a good tenderness. She worked the tired muscle till the ache eased, looking down across a body now brown, lean, smooth and strong as if all the muscles and tendons, sinews and bones had finally integrated. God knows she had arrived at Ed's lost and adrift, flesh soft and indulged. And now look at her, grounded deep into the earthen wonders of a physical presence she hadn't even been able to imagine back then. She flexed her muscles, loving the way she had at last taken residence in this body she was meant to dwell in, here in the outer world. A body she could depend upon when needed, with more capacity and resilience than she thought she would ever have to give.

*Patience knows nothing of time.* Another of Ed's favourites, which often came to mind when the land stretched out before her like this. How those few simple words always managed to ease her occasional drifts into anxiety about the future. She missed her dreaming now that it had taken second place to the deep tiredness of a full day's labour. But nothing was lost here. The harvest was nearly in. The coming summer would bring requests for dowsing as demand for water increased with the heat. She could hardly wait.

Kayla slipped into the driver's seat. It was a good three-hour round trip including shopping for groceries. She would pick up Ed at the top shed, since she still needed the company of a licensed driver to go to town. Planting her foot, she spun out of the paddock in a cloud of bulldust. Sometimes you just had to celebrate the best way you could.

Four months later, when Kayla finally got her licence two weeks after her eighteenth birthday, Ed presented her with a Holden ute all her own. Although well over ten years old, its mileage was low, and he figured she'd get a good run out of it. When she protested, Ed swore it had come from the extra harvest she was helping produce.

Days slipped into weeks through that summer. Ed worked her harder than ever, with the unspoken knowledge that this time together was reaching its natural end. Other places, travels and destinations had begun to enter their conversation.

It was thrilling and scary all at once, Kayla thought as she wandered down through the dawn-lit wetlands to the spring, needing to check the flow before she left. She crouched down and pulled back the moist layer of greenery that sheltered the opening. Hard to believe it was the last time, for now at least, that she would cup her hands and drink from this source. She'd been truly spoilt. Of all the bores and tanks, rivers and dams from which she'd drunk, only this spring and one other had held such purity and at the same time an essence of something so deeply earthen and ancient she didn't know how to describe it.

Kayla lay down in the cool, moist shade of the overhanging gums, some that Ed had planted, others that had grown of their own accord once safe haven was created – water truly brought life and never so clearly as in these deserts of inland Australia. Running the sandy soil through her fingers, breathing air pungent with drifting eucalyptus and the more immediate damp earthy flavour of plants she'd bruised upon entering this sanctuary, hearing the little wrens and finches singing their delight for the gift of longevity such an oasis provides, Kayla swallowed back a wave of emotion. She had never imagined how bonded she could become to this man and his spring and even these parched, denuded lands.

The decision had come on suddenly as they had talked late into the night. That in itself was unusual, as both of them so enjoyed early mornings that sleep was not hard to find once the sun had done its day. They had established early on that neither was interested in household chores, so basically each looked to their own. Kayla had just finished putting away her plate and cutlery and was setting up for a last cup of tea when Ed cleared his throat, the sound that often pre-empted something he didn't know how to say.

"So now you've got your car, I, ahh, guess you'll be heading off soon."

Kayla turned to face him, make sure she heard right. "What?"

"Well, you can't be staying here forever, and I just thought … now you've got wheels you'd want to be seeing more of the world than this old farm."

The grain of truth thing caught her lost for a reply. And he was right, it did represent a liberty she hadn't considered till she'd sat behind the wheel for the first time. But she had made no real plans yet, just dreaming. And it was too soon, she wasn't ready. Or was she? "Go where? Where do you think I should go?"

Ed laughed. "That's not up to me, girl. It's your life. Hell, all you need to do is drive away from here and the rest will take care of itself. What I wouldn't give to be eighteen again."

Kayla just stared at him, stricken. Surely he didn't really want her to go off without him … and just leave him here … on his own? Silence spread between them.

After a couple of minutes Ed spoke. "Time to let them old worries go, Kayla. They did you no service then and they'll do you none now. You're not the child that walked through that door anymore, and I've taken you as far as I can go. You have a talent it'd be wrong to stifle. And you have a life of loving to discover. I know, you've told me you're not interested in boys, but it doesn't mean you have to be alone." Ed caught her eye and nodded. "You hear me?"

Another grain of truth. Damn him, there was nothing she could argue against. "But where?" she asked again. Ed shook his head.

Kayla made the tea. "Alice's friend Barbara is heading to Tooleybuc on the bus. Maybe I could offer her a lift." Kayla meant it as a statement but could still hear the question in her voice.

"When does she want to leave?" Ed asked.

"End of week." It came out almost as a whisper.

"Well then, end of week it is," Ed said, just like that. "Send us a card when you get there. Won't have to think about you then."

There was such tenderness in the abrupt words it made Kayla smile, leaving her no choice but to respond with the intended spirit of the challenge. "All right, old man, I will. If I remember that is." Without giving him time to refuse she swooped in for a stolen hug from a man not easily affectionate. Kayla hoped he knew that she would miss him almost more than she could bear thinking about.

"Better go pack then, and give Alice a call. See you for breakfast." Kayla got out of there before he saw her tears. And she knew she wasn't the only one feeling it. It was after 2 a.m. before she heard Ed settle into the regular rhythm of his sleeping breath.

After a couple of nights in Tooleybuc, Kayla crossed the Murray River into New South Wales then headed north to Balranald. Here, in the dry dusty outback, the Murrumbidgie River meandered slowly between tall red sandy banks. Like the Murray, she was a defiant old river lined with stately, towering river gums, vibrant with birds and wildlife. It had been just the right thing to spend a precious few days camping out, getting used to being alone.

From there she turned east for the long journey to the coast. Every time she had tried to think of what to do next, images of the ocean washed through her mind. Now alone in the car, foot on the pedal, her heart sang with the rhythm of the ocean's song.

Like a series of stepping-stones reaching eastward from the Mallee all the way to the Pacific Ocean, Alice's women's network provided Kayla with the accommodation she needed. Barely a week later, Kayla followed the Hunter River from Muswellbrook down into Newcastle. A quick pass of the bustling, dirty coal port would be enough. Her swag had been fine for the dry outback but, anticipating the damp coastal weather, she picked up a back-up tent and a few necessities before turning north. Her intention was to hug the coast as best she could, but the scourge of coastal settlement and limited access kept forcing her inland. What a relief to finally drive through Yuraygir National Park and into the village of Minnie Water.

A couple of dirt tracks later, she found what she had dreamt of. A small grassy knoll topped a cliff that fell away to white sandy beaches disappearing further than she could see in each direction. Kayla stepped from the car into swirling wind that lifted off waves laden with spray. The stinging bite of salt and fresh ozone filled her nose and lungs, as she surrendered all thought to the relentless pounding beat of the thunderous roar rising from below. It may have been ten minutes, maybe it was an hour that she stood surrendering, softening, coming home. Fierce gusts buffeted her body. Had she been a kite she might just have flown away, swept into oblivion, liberated from the string that held her by the very forces that gave her purpose.

Here, where the land was only an edge to the ocean, her body swayed towards the water as if of its own volition. Oh, surely she had needed this more than anything else. She looked out, hungry for connection, across the ocean where for all she could tell, the next landing could be the island of her ancestors. Newfoundland. She rolled the word around in her mouth, timing it with the waves as they crashed on the shoreline below. "One day, maid," she promised into the wind, her words snatched as they were spoken. It didn't matter. Her intention was clear and resolute.

In a brief lull of the wind that came with dusk, Kayla set up her tent. She made a small fire within the protection of a horseshoe of piled rocks for just long enough to heat dinner and boil water for tea.

For the next week she only left the cliff top to take the steep path to the shoreline itself. Each day she walked for hours through the water's edge, following the reach of the tides as they ebbed and flowed. Sand and water churned around her bare feet, tumbling playfully as if animated with the same exuberant energy that excited her, the clear salty water as smooth and rounded as the pebbles and rocks caught in its grasp. Whether above or below, the roar was incessant. Each night, every sense saturated, she fell asleep to it, waking in the mornings to the thrill of its inescapable presence.

Then one morning it was time to go. She would remember this place and the respite she had found. It had cleared far more than just her head. The fine layer of encrusted salt she licked from her lips was a whole different taste from the heat-driven sweat of the last few years.

Kayla felt unexpectedly nervous as she pulled up at the Grafton address Beth had given her. Everywhere else she had stayed en route had been with people she'd known, if not personally, then culturally. Farming families who'd taken her in as they might have their own. Hard working, good people, often struggling to hang onto farms and properties either inherited or bought, still faithfully following the old practices, still believing that with enough hard work, the land would take care of its own.

Yet she had never doubted that she would come to this door.

# Chapter 9

"Shh. Keep your head down." They crept further along the chain-link fence. Muffled laughter came from the stragglers behind. Just ahead of her Kayla felt more than saw Beth stop and shake her head. "They're too stoned for this. Tell them to stay out and keep watch till we're done here."

Beth waited for Kayla's return, then one by one they slid through the fence where Jamie had cut the wire a few nights ago, opening access to seven properties backing onto the Richmond River. Tonight they were gathering water samples from discharge pipes all the way upriver to where the last factory outlet flowed unchecked into the water. At the last minute Lucas, Chris and Eva had decided to join in, offering to leave a written commentary across the cold concrete faces of the factory walls. Despite their intoxication, as a cohesive team they had worked fast. Let the River Live; Let Our Children Drink Clean Water; and Rivers Are the Veins of the Earth were already scrawled across the walls in bright primary colours.

All other forms of protest had yielded little result, with rarely even the courtesy of a reply. The plan was to flood the relevant departments, company boards, shareholders, and the media with a constant stream of clearly labelled samples and reports until they could no longer be ignored.

Kayla held back as Beth bottled another sample from an industrial laundry. It had been a harrowing night for Kayla, her guts churning every step of the way. The current legislation regulating waste disposal was lenient, the Environmental Protection Authority ineffective beyond letters of recommendation and insignificant fines. Most of the businesses here in this small regional town had responded to calls to clean up their act in support of the long-term fishing and tourism opportunities. But, as always, a few greedy rogue operators continued to take full advantage, pumping out sludge like there was no tomorrow. And there wouldn't be if something wasn't done, so they were doing something.

Beth and Kayla snuck back out and made their way further upstream. Muted sounds of conversation carried on the breeze. It was nearly done, only three samples to go.

That was when they heard a click, followed by another. Metallic sounds, out of place.

"Car door," Kayla whispered. Beth nodded as they both lowered their bodies into the greasy slick of mud and weeds. There was no way they could warn the others, but the sudden silence gave them hope that they had heard it too.

The sound of boots on gravel echoed as torch beams crisscrossed the empty factory yards. The security or police were making a thorough job of it. Someone must have seen the fresh graffiti slogans. That was good. They needed to raise public awareness any which way they could.

In unspoken agreement, Kayla and Beth slithered silently over the side of the bank into the black water, pulling themselves along on loose roots until they reached an earthen overhang they could slip under and still have room to breathe. The water was a toxic putrid brew of god knows what.

"It's as bad as we thought." Kayla shuddered, giddy with the pain of the water. Beth knew enough to keep a strong arm safely around Kayla till they were back on shore.

"Hey you! What are you doing here?" The shout came from above. The pounding of fleeing footsteps took off in several directions, then silence again. "Damn. Looks like they got away."

Beth and Kayla were close enough to share a smile. It was hard not to giggle. The escape plans they had discussed before leaving seemed to have worked; the others had slipped away. After the searchers left, Beth finished the last few sites with Kayla stumbling along behind.

Back at the house, Kayla drained the hot water tank, scalding the residue of the filthy river and its memory out of her skin. Now all she needed was a warm drink before bed.

"You OK?" Beth asked as Kayla entered the kitchen. Kayla was surprised to see her still up till she saw the papers spread out across the table. Beth was so damn dedicated, compulsive, obsessive even, and times like these Kayla worried for her friend.

"Yeah, I'm good. Or will be soon enough. But what's all this? I thought you would be in bed by now."

"Oh, you know, someone's got to do it." They shared a smile.

Truth was, Kayla knew that compulsion better than most. "OK then," she said, sliding onto one of the empty chairs. "Let's have it."

Kayla felt a wave of gratitude wash over her as Beth took a moment to look at her over the top of her glasses before beginning. Kayla knew only too well what long, lonely, arduous tasks these could be and was happy to help.

"So, truth is that even with all we've done, things are barely better than they were. I've just been going through the grant applications and yes, Wilson's Laundry installed that recycling plant and sure, it's great that they're feeding clean water into the park watering system. And even Ben's Bakery is finally diverting their waste products. But I don't know, Kayla. It's so damn frustrating. No one wants to pay for change, and there's no way I can find funds for everybody. Trying to juggle all these crappy, stingy grants – it's never going to be enough. And you can bet this round of testing won't inspire anyone." Beth shook her head, tossed her glasses onto the table and rubbed her eyes. "I'm just tired is all. I'll be alright tomorrow."

Knowing how burnt out her friend was, it was impossible to know what to offer without sounding even a little bit critical. "Maybe we could try another approach as well," Kayla suggested gently, waiting till Beth looked up and leaned back in her chair.

"Go on," she said.

This was good. With a deep breath Kayla stepped boldly into the opening. "I was thinking about one of Ed's favourites while we were hiding in the river earlier. Whenever a business tried to cheat him or disrespect his work he'd say 'When all else fails, hit them in their wallet.' Then he'd never do business with them again, stubborn old bastard he was."

Even Beth chuckled at that. He still had it! How Kayla loved the rebellious spirit of this black sheep of the family. Ed had given her so much but there was still more to this thought.

"He truly believed if we all did this, companies would have to listen. I remember him adding something like, 'To survive, capitalism has to keep expanding, consuming everything in its path, and convince you to do the same. To them, nothing is sacred or safe. If we all refused to buy into the game, it would eat its very own, like the worst of the monsters ever imagined by humankind. Never forget that this is the vulnerable underbelly of a system that needs you and I to play, that needs you far more than you need it.'"

Beth nodded. "Yeah, I like that. I like that a lot."

"Me too. Now we've just got to find a way to get right under their skin."

The grin they shared was full of mischief and possibility and together they spent the next few hours sorting through papers and tossing around ideas. Kayla kept thinking about Ed. How grateful she was for the way he had sharpened her perceptions and encouraged her to find her own way.

And maybe she had still been naïve and unworldly when she arrived here among Beth's dynamic urban crew. But really, it hadn't taken too long before she'd learnt how to share in their banter. Unlike many in this opinionated group, she tried to listen first, and consider what had been said, rather than focus on her own clever answer. After a while they had begun to listen and value her contributions. That had been scary! Hardest part was when she had come to realise that there was a level of cynicism, of frustrated hopelessness underpinning their choices for confrontation and retribution that deeply troubled her. And still did. It was so hard to know what to do.

Finally exhaustion put an end to the night. Minutes later she was snuggled up in bed, worn out but glad to have been part of the testing.

Uneasy dreams came in the early hours. Anxious and fretting, Kayla tossed and turned till finally woken by clammy, febrile sweat soaking her shirt. After changing she was soon drawn back into restless sleep.

Nunik came just before dawn. Gladly Kayla followed her lead, diving down into deep green, refreshingly cold, clear clean water. Lower and lower they plunged, weaving through a dense forest of swaying seaweed, till they reached the ocean floor. Huge rocks lay strewn through giant kelp as if in ages past a mountain had crumbled and fallen over a great distance. Indicating Kayla to join her, Nunik swam into a deep hollow in one of the fallen boulders, a pond within a pond. How could a girl resist?

Reaching for a cluster of fine sea-grass, soft and ethereal as gossamer, Nunik began to swab the scourge of fevered heat from Kayla's body. She closed her eyes, ceding to the relief that followed in the wake of each soothing stroke, vaguely aware that she now lay with her head on Nunik's lap, nestled into the soft, generous folds of her round belly. The last thing she remembered was opening her eyes only to be lost in the timeless depths of Nunik's own. Nunik continued to stroke Kayla's forehead with such unbridled tenderness she almost cried with the joy of it. Like a mantra, *It is only change, everything is going to be all right* ran in a loop through her mind. Then, in a blink, it was morning.

As part of the collective of resistance, Kayla wrote impassioned letters, attended marches, actions and sit-ins. It was surprisingly reassuring to attend rallies – to be one of five, fifty or, for one exceptional event supporting Indigenous land rights, fifty thousand voices brought together as one in shared dissent. For ten memorable days she joined twenty-five other women from all over Australia on the Murray River near Barmah, locked to logging machinery to protest the ongoing felling of the largest river red gum forest in the world.

But it wasn't the answer.

Half a year had passed when, one morning, Kayla found Beth alone in the kitchen. It was a rare opportunity – with Beth's growing commitments and the full and busy household there were few such moments. It was time to broach the idea that had been floating in her mind.

"I've been wondering what to do for the next few years. I'm thinking of going to uni in Brisbane. But I'm not sure."

Beth looked up from her breakfast. "To study what?"

"Oh, you know. Something to do with water, I guess." Kayla smiled.

"Of course." Beth returned the smile.

Kayla loved the way Beth totally got it. "I know these things we do make a difference, developing awareness and some sense of responsibility. But it's not enough. We're just banging on the walls of a system that's got no room for compassion, or empathy, or connection. They don't care. But it's not a place I can continue to dwell in." She fumbled with the kettle, suddenly close to tears. "So maybe I need to try another way. How else are we really going to be heard without the 'appropriate' academic background? Maybe we need to become the 'voices of authority', to be acknowledged by the powers that be."

"Maybe. But science is already being shut out of the debate. Corporations don't want to hear anything that slows the momentum." Beth shook her head. "I don't know, Kayla. I see your struggle, and I feel the same frustrations. But I can't begin to imagine you fitting into their parameters. You're a water-empath, Kayla. Your gift is already more relevant to the world than all the learning you could do. Have you checked out the courses yet?"

Kayla nodded. "There's one in hydrology. It's four years studying the water systems of the world. How it's distributed, how it occurs, how it moves and its uses. All stuff that I'm interested in. But the emphasis seems to be on human use – use being the word that worries me. Also, I would likely be the only woman in the course."

"Yeah, that's true. And you'd probably spend the rest of your days standing against those very same classmates." Beth's disdain and distrust resonated in her voice. "But if you really think you could handle all that, and use it to make a difference, maybe it would be worth it."

Kayla shook her head. "That's the thing. The course is already biased. Even the section that deals with pollutants and the consequences of contamination seems to be focused on solutions after the harm was done. They basically accept collateral damage as just what happens. I'm worried I'd end up feeling more like a co-conspirator."

"There you go then. You have your own answer." They sat with that a while before Beth reached across the table and took Kayla's hands in her own. "Remember what Ed said about you being a translator?"

Kayla nodded.

"He was right, Kayla. It's who you are. You already know more about the nature of water than any lectures could offer. I've loved having you here, but I guess you have what you came for." Beth squeezed Kayla's hands as her eyes glistened. "Kayla, you are a sister of my soul and have taught me more than you can ever imagine with your gentle truthful heart. Sometimes you seem as damn near uncontaminated as those precious springs you so love. Our struggle here is dirty and despairing and I would never want you to feel as jaded as I find myself some days. Don't become like us."

Kayla squeezed back, silenced by the truth of the words that only strengthened their bond, and by the imminent loss that was forming as they spoke. She could see in Beth's eyes that she wasn't the only one feeling it.

"I think what you do, Beth, the way you inspire and unite people, is incredibly important. Sometimes I wonder if in another lifetime, or maybe as my alter ego, I would stay, doing just what you do. But then … knowing you are here … it helps me leave, lets me follow this other path. You're right, I can't explore this thing weighted down by the frustration and disappointment you wake to every day. But hear me, Beth … when I say just how grateful I am that you will go on doing what I can't."

Beth looked up with a happy sad smile. "Thanks, Kayla. So go then, get on out of here and do what you must. Free yourself, little fish. Travel the rivers, speak with the oceans and waterfalls. Then speak for them. Find the language to translate the love we can only show in our actions. And – if you can, take a bit of me with you." Beth's voice caught on her last words.

Kayla came round the table to hug her friend. "You will always be part of who I am," she whispered into Beth's soft hair.

# Chapter 10

Kayla roamed the eastern coastline, beach by beach, river by river. She took jobs where she could get them, in the kitchens of restaurants, tending bars, some seasonal fruit picking. Now and then, following a recommendation from Ed or his cronies, she would turn inland, travelling hundreds of kilometres to locate a new water source for a well or bore. Drought held much of the interior in rainless suspension, stock perished and crops withered back into dust. But the occasional win, even on a small scale, was life-changing, sometimes life-saving, for those involved.

On days when she wasn't working, she took picnics up tributaries, rewarded with the rare experience of reaching a source as it bled from a cleft or a spring. Feeling the water as it skidded and fell free and trusting over boulders and cliffs, how it was before and then after the drop, how some pools rested and others stewed in tainted discomfort, she began to keep a daily log dedicated to these forays and how each touch spoke of its passage.

Everywhere she went had the same common denominator. Every tract of land touched by human contact was endangered by the experience. Contaminated waste and runoff from farming and factories, mining and urbanisation, were flowing unchecked into surface and underground water. Short-term interests were putting the long-term welfare of whole river systems at risk.

The surest way to support the health of the host was to nourish the blood and, in Kayla's thinking, in the case of the planet this meant caring for the waterways that reached like veins into every far corner. Everything else was background noise to the rallying call she heard in the weary rhythm of dust-heavy rain, and in the lonely sigh of moisture-laden wind.

From notice boards and contacts she made, Kayla tapped into local community meetings and interest groups. She attended those concerned with issues of water and conservation. Mostly she just listened.

Groups were strange creatures, Kayla thought as she sat in on a meeting of bird-lovers concerned by the degradation of local wetlands. Each group developed into a unique entity reflecting the combination of its highly individual parts. People without opinions rarely attended meetings, so those present always had plenty to say. Most gatherings were earnest and passionate, which she liked, some strangled by control. Others were rowdy and chaotic, and if they didn't rapidly implode, she found these were often the most dynamic, creative and inspiring.

Hard not to miss Beth and the life in the shared house. It was the first like-minded tribe she had dwelt among. It had done her good, re-socialising with peers, not just those of age but with those searching for connection, a household of young people awake to, and willing to take part in, the importance of choices being made on their behalf. Though she would find temporary sanctuary in houses such as these scattered throughout the country, she learnt it was a small percentage of the population that gave a damn enough to act.

This made her happier though, moving about as the whim took her, as if she crept under a protective canopy from forest to forest, alone, unseen, with the inherent stealth of her ancestors, except when she chose to be noticed. At Beth's she'd been reminded that she liked people, but not all the time. Truth was, she liked the companionship of nature more that anyone she met.

Far from those dry corridors of power and learning that had almost tempted her in, she continued to seek the people on the ground dealing with the realities of the times. From trickling rivers to empty dams, from filthy creeks to stagnant ponds, drained wetlands to ravaged springs, Kayla followed a growing trail of communities and individuals forced to take a stand. Overcoming her natural reserve, she introduced herself where she thought she could make a difference. Her capacity to locate waterways, intuit their condition, and then share this innate knowing was already exceptional. Yet always there was a sense that there was more.

Even as her experience and reputation grew, Kayla was still surprised and touched by the unpredictable connections made by word-of-mouth networks as they rippled across the country. Two years earlier she had successfully dowsed for Rob and Wendy, a couple from Mitchell in regional Queensland. She was now in Nanango, nearly five hundred kilometres east, where Wendy's distant cousin, Damien, had a macadamia and lychee farm, now under threat from an unnatural degradation.

Government environmental representatives had been reassuring the locals that there was nothing "notably significant" affecting their water supply, but the farmers were not convinced. Crops were slow and haphazard, and it wasn't just the weather. There had been complaints about headaches, nausea and above-average immune system weaknesses.

Without hard evidence, government authorities were not prepared to proceed further, and the community had found the costs of self-funding prohibitive. After much persuasion, Damien's local farming group, concerned that it must be the quality of their irrigation water, had at last agreed to bring Kayla to Nanango to investigate. Kayla had heard their story and was happy to do what she could just for board and keep.

There was only one way to begin the search. Starting from the nearest recognised problematic site, she would hike upriver as far as the day allowed, find a crossing and return along the opposite bank. Having arrived the night before it was with backpack in hand that she made her way downstairs into the kitchen in the early dawn.

"Morning to you," said Damien, busy at the stove. Turning, he indicated with a bubbling, crackling pan towards another guest at the table. "Kayla, this is Dee, she lives upriver. Thought you might be glad of a guide today. No one knows that area like she does."

Kayla turned to Dee, immediately liking the unassuming warmth of this woman's soft brown eyes. "I'd be glad for the company," she responded, and was reassured by the grateful nod of acceptance she received.

Before she had time to speak further, Damien was at her side loading her plate with steaming eggs and bacon, tomatoes and mushrooms. Kayla loved the way country folk ate, every meal a celebration of the bounty they had played a part in producing. How weary she'd become of the picky eaters of the city, with their self-absorbed disdain for the very sustenance their scrawny bodies needed. It was almost an insult to the efforts of these farmers and their gifts garnered from this dry, reluctant dirt.

Kayla tucked into the hearty fare, listening to these friends catching up on news. There was a shared history here, a mutual respect for the individual struggle of lives dedicated to nourishing more than their own tables.

Dee offered to drive, and they climbed into a well-worn old Kombi van, sweet with the familiar scent of freshly cut hay. There were two bales in the back and an assortment of tools and materials which, Kayla noted with an experienced eye, would cover most contingencies.

Along the way they drove through wide flat fields, some lush with the disturbing luminous green perkiness of chemical farming, others the barren fields of broken-down farms, clearly depleted by the harrowing practices of traditional agriculture till the dust just blew away. Growing clusters of smaller hobby farms came next, clinging to the edge of the narrow coastal green belt.

"So, who's the feed for?" Kayla asked, indicating the bales behind her.

"Oh, you know, pigs, sheep, chickens and all the other members of the strange and diverse family of creatures with whom I share this wonderful life," Dee replied with a cheeky lift of an eyebrow.

"Do tell." Kayla laughed. "Sounds like just the story to pass the miles."

"OK, seeing as you asked," Dee replied with a grin. "You know, it's hard to believe it's more than twenty-five years since I first came here looking for sanctuary, searching for somewhere wild and peaceful." She glanced over at Kayla. "Now I'm guessing that, like me, when you look out there all you see is ravaged land. Cleared then overstocked year after year, its watercourses trampled into terrible bogs." Dee frowned before gesturing out the window. "All this is regrowth – and sure it's great to see but you can't imagine how heart wrenching it was back then, and so desperate for renewal. I couldn't just drive on by. It took a couple of months, but in the end I was lucky enough to find a hidden pocket upstream that still held some of that magic I searched for. A hundred and eighty-eight acres, bankrupt and bereft. Picked it up for a pittance, and that's where I've been ever since, coaxing it back to life."

There was a deep satisfaction in Dee's voice, but from her own time in the Mallee, Kayla knew all too well the depth of vulnerability of these denuded plains and the immense effort it had taken to restore this country. Despite the apparent harshness, these vast tracts of fringe land were unbelievably fragile. What a commitment this woman had made. Kayla wanted to know more. "Go on," she said.

"Well, I admit I was pretty compulsive at first, driven I suppose, but I had to do whatever I could to stop the last of the topsoil from blowing away. Where there was enough dirt I seeded native grasses, and a mixture of shrubs and sapling trees. Twenty a week for the first two years and now we almost have a forest with the shade and protection that the poor soil needed. She can be a mighty hot land out here." Dee stopped and nodded, almost to herself. "In closer to the house I planted fruit and nut orchards, between heavily mulched gardens, where we now produce most of our food."

What a task. No wonder she was tired. "Who's we?" Kayla asked.

Dee chuckled. "Good question. My only answer that it's all of us. All the entities – plant, animal and even human, me being the only one of those at this time, who have chosen to dwell on this precious piece of land in this time and space." Dee nodded and laughed and took a quick glance at Kayla, adding "And I am thinking you might just understand what I mean," before turning her attention back to the road.

She did indeed! She'd known immediately that there was much she would like about this woman.

It was short time later that Dee pointed out her mailbox, an old tin drum marking a driveway that led up over a rise that blocked Kayla's view. From there on the country became harsher, drier by the kilometre. She'd heard rainfall could drop an inch a mile as you turned inland and this sure looked like one of those situations. The bitumen gave way to dirt, and Kayla was impressed how Dee and her Kombi van handled the deteriorating track before it turned into churned ruts only a four-wheel drive could handle.

The thirty-odd kilometres to where they would leave the van passed in a minute, or so it seemed to Kayla. She hadn't enjoyed company or a conversation like that in a long time. An older woman, clearly used to her own company and counsel, Dee's thinking was eclectic, expansive and well informed.

"You know we've already done this, time and again, till we've fair worn out the trail. There's nothing we've been able to see," Dee muttered as they pulled over. She was probably right. Kayla's experience told her it was most likely something they couldn't see.

To their left the land ran away to a vague haze; the red, rocky, slightly undulating surface broken only by a scattering of stunted, hardy scrub. To their right was Sandy Creek, cloaked by an avenue of tall, deep-rooted old gums, scant remnants of life once sustained. The contrast was as extreme as the merciless heat that in summer burned the exposed stone black.

Leaving the van, they followed a narrow foot track down to the tree line. Kayla didn't have to touch the water to recognise the queasiness in her gut. There was still a good flow to the river, but there was very little green in the grasses and reeds that lined the banks and shallows. Regardless of the needs downstream, they had to find the problem. These lowly, rarely acknowledged plants were all that held the river on its current course, securing the integrity of the soil during the merciless ravages of flooding rains and storms.

Barely fifty metres along, the river disappeared through a gap between twin hills. "It's a climb from here. But there's a bit of a treat the other side of this escarpment," Dee said with a strange sort of happy sad look.

It was always surprising how quickly these desert hills rose. From the top, Kayla could follow the canopy of trees that accompanied the river as it dwindled into the far distant haze. But below was even more unexpected. In a pocket formed by a circle of seven such hills was a hidden pool, ringed by such a palette of greens she had to wonder if every species of vulnerable native plant had left genes in this sanctuary.

Making their way down through a steep bank of ferns, Kayla and Dee came to a pool fed by three tributary streams. Although the sun shone brightly, it was cool and fresh beneath the leafy cover. Little wrens and finches fluttered through the branches, but something was not right. Kayla could feel it in her blood, a sensation she had learnt to dread.

"It's up past here, Dee," she called out. "We'll have to go up further." But which feeder stream was it? Stripping to her bathers, Kayla slipped down into the water.

She swam through the sparkling water to the cascades that brought each creek tumbling into the pool. When she approached the third and smallest, she gasped. There it was. The slight tingling she'd felt since entering the water was turning into sharp abrasions as if someone had taken to her skin with coarse sandpaper.

Then the shards rushed through her veins, taking her breath. She swam over to the far bank, swept handfuls of cleaner water over her skin then scoured her body with the dry towel.

"This is it," Kayla said, nodding at Dee. "It's coming down through here. It doesn't seem to have a smell, and nothing I could taste. And it's as clear as the rest, but …"

"It makes me so mad," Dee muttered, and shook her head. "Those government bastards already looked up through here and keep telling us there's nothing wrong. We told them months ago. And look here" – she pointed – "how brown it is. Anyone could see that it's dying back."

Kayla sat down on the soft bank, encouraging Dee to do the same. "I know it's hurting, but let's take a moment to just sit. What a sanctuary this is. It must be just about in your backyard, Dee."

"Pretty much. Though I've never felt that my responsibility ends at my fence line. This is our backyard, all of us. How could they do this?"

Kayla closed her eyes. Dee was right. How could they? This wasn't the first time she'd come to a place such as this, a rare oasis surrounded by desolate plains in every direction. How revered this gem must be to the traditional owners when they came this way, and how respectful they would be of its pristine state.

Drawing on the moist misty air, she let the gurgling music of the cascades wash over her till she was lost to the song. Two out of three of the tributaries were clean and so this is where she would stay, psychically bathing till the taint of despair was dispelled. She had learnt she needed to do this. Days searching for darkness could pile despair upon despair until she could hardly bear the weight. She couldn't risk going under, dumped by the waves of hopelessness that emanated from those whose lives were changing.

*The one certainty in life is change.* Ed's words resonated with their simple truth. *But what a gift that is,* was how he always completed it with a chuckle. And another time: *If we are part of nature then we are born with the same innate resilience.* He had taught her that by not resisting change you could be flexible, adapting like nature always had and always would long after we were gone, evolving to meet the altered circumstances without the fear of loss so paralysing to the human mind. He had shown her trees ravaged by bushfire, others struck by lightning, all of which had grown beyond their wounds into stately old matriarchs of the forests. And he had shown her ancient riverbeds, where once great waters flowed, that had evolved into thriving desert communities for whom water was a rare memory.

Dee took a sample before they continued up the creek. Wary of the water, Kayla stayed on the bank. There was no track, and the bush was thick and entangled, the going getting harder. Thank goodness they had brought their own water.

An hour further in, they were both more than ready to throw in the towel when something changed. All of a sudden the discomfort that had plagued Kayla since the pool eased. By another thirty metres the sharp abrasiveness was gone altogether. She dipped her fingers. That was better. The water was smooth again, sparkling and exuberant. She cupped her hand and drank what was now clear, untarnished nectar.

"We've gone past it," Kayla said. "Give us your water bottle and I'll top them up."

"But we didn't see anything. What the hell's going on?" Dee said.

Kayla shrugged. "Guess we'll find out soon enough," she added, trying to sound hopeful. They sat and ate lunch, each lost to their own thoughts till Kayla stood.

"Let's head back to where it starts again. There's got to be something here, we just have to find it."

It wasn't hard at all to locate the point of change. As they closed in, Kayla began to feel a throb in her direction, a brittle pulse of distress. If only she carried some kind of diviner like her dowsing rods – but all she had was instinct. She closed her eyes, letting her mind clear, turning till she lurched forward, as if suddenly pulled towards the object of her intent.

Drawn and repulsed at the same time, for several hundred yards Kayla followed the lead into a patch of dense scrub. Even before the bush opened up, she knew they were there. Knew it was much more than the heat that was making her woozy as a cold clammy sweat crept over her body.

They stepped out onto a rough-hewn track that came from nowhere. Following it to its end they reached a deep slash of erosion, a hidden ravine some five metres deep. Dozens of containers big and small, some plastic, others metal, lay as they'd fallen, discarded in disarray along the gully floor. From previous experience Kayla was more prepared for what they had found. But it still was shocking.

"Bloody hell!" was all Dee could say as she scanned the horror laid out before her.

They slid down on loose gravel until they reached the bottom. Kayla pulled out a couple of pairs of gloves and handed a set to Dee. "Don't touch anything directly, but let's see if we can find any labels." But as she had suspected, there were none. Nothing to describe what was in the containers nor from where they had come. With the high cost of the disposal of toxic wastes, hidden illegal dumps were a booming black-market business.

It didn't take long to find two drums with liquid seeping through rusted rims.

"Bet these are the culprits." Kayla crouched carefully and poked at the sticky brown stain with a stick. "Looks like this sludge has been seeping down through the soil into the underground water system and then out into the creek. Give us a hand to turn them, Dee. Maybe only one side's rusted."

Together they rolled the barrels over. Fortunately they were still intact enough to hold till help could be arranged.

"It's hard to imagine how these toxins turned up on your farms till you understand that about a quarter of our rainfall soaks through into the underground waterways, taking everything dissolvable and anything else it can carry with it. This here is an extreme version, but there's an immeasurable amount of the crap we leave on the earth's surface and pump into the air that enters the cycle this way. Rain forms around particles, so whatever we send up will eventually rain down upon us again."

It was a horrific scene, but at least they'd found it for all concerned. But Kayla knew there was no immediate relief for Dee. Her farm and community still had the consequences and the clean-up to deal with. Sometimes, depending on the nature of the contamination, it could affect the region for years to come. Carefully, they took further samples and made their way back. Kayla's part was done, and at least they now had proof that they hoped would force the authorities to act.

This was a turning point for Kayla. For the first time she had recognised the point of intrusion as if the water itself had spoken. There was no denying her growing affinity; that the water in her veins was linked to the water of the earth as if of the same body. That when the rivers hurt, so did she.

There had never really been a choice, touched as she was with this inherent empathy. What else could she do? All those dreams had been leading her here. And all the academic degrees and other worldly recognition she might achieve would never equal this truth. This was her offering.

The idea was exhausting. The work would be full of times like today when her whole being ached. Later that day, as she restored her equilibrium to the happy murmur of an untainted tributary, a familiar peace came upon her. For her, as for this stream, somewhere out there was the ocean, the final resting place she would reach when her work was done, and her life over. Like a droplet separated at birth she would come home to join with the great body that in the end encompasses all. But for now she would honour the gift with commitment. Kayla woke the next morning with such a clear sense of purpose that it was months before the deep tiredness came upon her again.

But it did, time and time again, with humans becoming more careless and modern life more toxic. River systems all over her country, all over the world, were sickening, pouring tainted water into oceans as if it had endless capacity to cleanse and renew. In the frantic pursuit of fossil fuels and minerals, contamination was spreading like a rash the earth could never scratch and rarely heal.

The odds were stacking up against the dedicated warriors like Beth who stood up for one precious pocket of country at a time. But for Kayla? It had never been clearer that in years to come wars would not be fought over fossil fuels as they had been, but over sources of fresh, clean water.

# *Chapter 11*

*Damn them. Damn them all!* Even the music wasn't doing it. Usually hitting the road with the stereo turned up and the anticipation of fresh adventure was enough. But not this time. Yet again her efforts had been wasted, her appeal powerless and ineffectual, even after she had pinpointed the contamination from badly regulated pesticides so clearly. Always the same story: water rights violated, legislation specifically aimed at commodifying natural resources regardless of consequence. So what now? All that for nothing? Kayla thumped the steering wheel with her fists. It hadn't been enough. *She* hadn't been enough.

And now she had to drive north to Tully, twelve hundred kilometres, and that was if she went straight up the highway. Kayla groaned. Travelling highways felt like following the threads of settlement from which the devastation unwound.

Bloody hell, she was tired, and suddenly she couldn't stop a torrent of frustrated tears that came on the wave of grief she'd held back since driving away.

A bridge crossing appeared ahead. Braking quickly, Kayla pulled off the road. It was hard to see through the scrub to what lay below. *Please, please let there be water*, she begged as she slid down an embankment steeper than she would have liked. Desperation drove her as she pushed through the blackberries at the bottom. Then there it was, a narrow but steady stream, gurgling its way over rocks and through forest debris, bubbling, oxygenating and restoring the only way it knew how.

Stripping her shoes and pants, Kayla waded in to a sandy shoal where she could sit in the caress of the cool clear water. Till the voices of despair faded. Till there was nothing but the song of the water as it made its way to the sea.

Sometime later, dried and dressed and back in the car, Kayla reviewed her map. Maybe she could take a meandering route, one that would take her by every river and waterway and though every reserve and forest she could justify. She breathed deeply, trying to keep the calm she had just found. Folding up the map, she smiled, anticipating at least some joy in the journey, joy that she hadn't felt for far too long.

Leonie and Pete, old friends of Beth's, had called last week. The couple had settled on a small acreage of remnant rainforest some twenty kilometres out of Tully. Looking for a simple alternative lifestyle, they had hoped to raise a few cattle and pigs and grow their own veggies, supplemented with native edible fauna and fish from the river.

It was not to be. Despite abundant water the vegetable garden was failing to thrive. In the last two years only one sow had managed to reach term and produce live piglets. Plant life along the river had died back as if burnt, but it was the silence of nights devoid of frog song that had forced them to reach out for help.

Once on site it didn't take long for Kayla to locate the main source of contamination as several runoff channels that drained from extensive sugarcane farming enterprises upriver.

"Let's sit here for a bit." Kayla patted the ground beside her after spotting a little patch of green, untainted life on the embankment. They needed a moment before returning home. At least Leonie did.

Leonie sat. Silent. Shocked. Kayla had seen this before, even when they had known it was coming. When that moment of truth stole a person's words as surely as it had stolen the future.

"What can we do?" Leonie asked eventually. "There's nothing, is there?"

Kayla shook her head. "No there's not, Leonie. Nothing that will change things for your family."

They sat a while longer. "Is it worth asking them to stop?" Leonie turned to Kayla, eyes brimming with angry unshed tears.

What could she say? There was no happy answer, no solution. The problem was spiralling out of control. Corporations were out of control.

"You could try, but …" Kayla shook her head. "My experience is that no one wants to talk, let alone change practices, and really there's no one to insist. Sad as it is, I think I would just get the hell out of here while you still can."

Leonie stared at her then, as if finally seeing the truth in her eyes, turned back to look across the yellowing fields. "And go where? This is like a war against nature. How do we do this? How do we keep the children safe?"

Kayla drew a deep breath fighting her own grief, her own fears and the brittle fragility deep in her soul. "Go somewhere upriver, Leonie. Go closer to the source where the river runs clean and hang on to it for dear life. I don't know how, or if, we are ever going to stop this madness. Go and create a refuge. I think we're going to need sanctuary in the days to come more than we can even imagine right now."

There on the bank they shared a long hug and a sad smile. Kayla ached for this young woman, for the loss of her dreams and trust in the illusion of safety that carried many people through life without too much fear for days to come. Life would never be the same for this young family, and she could only wish them the best as they put their farm up for sale the following week.

Over the next weeks Kayla took it upon herself to monitor the other creeks and rivers in this predominantly sugarcane-growing region. Evidence was everywhere of the impact of the chemical regimes applied over the growing season. Right across the Herbert River, Tully and Johnstone River districts, freshwater wetlands were disappearing in direct relationship to drainage works for the sugar industry.

Anyone she asked, especially the old codgers she found fishing along riverbanks, told her fish numbers were down. The very thought of eating the tainted fish turned her stomach, yet whenever Kayla tried to introduce the subject, her words were met with shrugs of indifference. It seemed most people figured that with the massive rainfall statistics that Tully boasted, any problem would be diluted or completely washed away. *But to where?* she'd ask silently, teeth clenched, hands curled tight with frustration. Where do you think it bloody well goes? Mars?

After finding a sensitive, sympathetic ear in Michael Thomas, a fourth-generation cane farmer out of Cardwell, Kayla was able to put a name to the type of pesticide that was the likely cause of Leonie and Pete's despair. Michael was determined not to be the last in his line to farm, adapting his crop practices to nurture a long-term sustainable outcome.

"Here." He wrote down the names of several popular herbicides. "These are the latest super chemicals around these parts. Won't have a bar of them myself."

Kayla took samples upstream from Leonie and Pete's property, and funded the tests herself. High levels of a widely promoted herbicide, a chemical brew that was suspected of being an endocrine disrupter that interfered with hormonal activity, were present, along with a bunch of other nasties. She sent the results to several government departments but to no avail.

There was no real difference between this experience, the one before or the one before that. Gloom settled over Kayla, a dark shadow she couldn't shrug off. Some part of her had reached a limit, the thought of dealing with another broken family or farm caught in another toxic trap by another ruthless corporation more than she could bear.

It was bad enough that every investigation was exposing her physical body to villainous concoctions, but it was the fractured, brittle water itself that was sometimes so sharp and harsh that afterwards she checked for abrasions on her skin. Connected as she was, it was like being immersed in a brew of a billion irreparably damaged innocents, and knowing, as with children, that the damage never quite goes away. Some find the resilience and grace to live beyond it. Some don't. Either way, memory remains. Reluctantly, Kayla was being forced to acknowledge the weighty residue in her own watery cells, and it was breaking her heart. She was yet to meet another like herself, and if she couldn't do it then who could? This path so full of hope and justice had become a lonely, harrowing road of futility.

When a friend offered the use of an old shack behind Mission Beach, Kayla took it up without hesitation, desperately needing to retreat and recover. A warm and gentle sea lay cradled between the mainland and the distant coral islands of the Great Barrier Reef. Day after day, surrendering to an instinctive need, Kayla immersed her pummelled body in the soft, buoyant water, seeking the most pristine pockets she could find. Till she began to find trust. Till one morning her body didn't flinch with anxious anticipation of risking contact with splintered water.

Savouring the strengthening of her body, Kayla swam out deeper into the reef-protected waters. The coral harboured a wonderland of sea life: every day a kaleidoscope of colour, form and movement, a complex interwoven system of mutual survival playing out below the surface.

How beautiful and heart-filling it was. Even the death zones of bleached-out coral and sea debris, so clearly related to the locations of mainland drains and marinas, were not enough to steal the magic. In a deliberate strategy of self-preservation, Kayla looked away. They would still be there when she was ready. But first she needed to reclaim her wonder.

In the meditative state of floating face down for hours, snorkelling in the balmy blue tropical waters, she began to remember her dreaming. Not so much the visions but the feeling of oneness, as though her skin no longer held her separate. She hadn't realised how disconnected she had become. As if the darkness of her tasks had closed the portals, it was now months since her dreams had transported her to those lands of rock and ice and turbulent deep green oceans.

How she missed Nunik. Even more than family. If only she knew how to reach for her again. But there had been so little time to mourn her loss. Truth was that she was scared that she might lose herself somewhere in the middle, caught between an almost overwhelming sense of responsibility and enough self-awareness to know that immersion in the work she'd taken on was depleting something deep within her.

Kayla decided to spend her last day as far from land as she could. Revelling in the sleek power of her refreshed body, she swam the kilometre and a half to the nearest atoll. It was barely fifteen metres across, but it was landfall and private and, for just this time, hers alone. The sun was gentle as it dried the moisture from her skin, leaving it painted with a pale salty residue. For the first time in a while she could truly say she felt happy, peace-filled and replete.

She felt it before she heard it, heard it before she saw it. Just beyond where her bare toes dug into golden sand, where the coral fell away into the deep blue of sudden depths, the broad, lustrous silver back of a dolphin broke through the surface. Streams of glistening water fell away, clearing the dolphin's blowhole just long enough for it to draw breath before it returned to the deep. One after the other a pod of a dozen long sleek humpback dolphins passed the atoll, some breaching, others twisting and playing, effortlessly filling her heart with the presence of their immensity and power. Charismatic life-affirming energy washed over her in irrepressible ecstatic waves till she was breathless with laughter. Then, with one final concerted leap, they were gone.

Tears flowed down her cheeks, falling onto the sand, running into the ocean, the accumulated grief of the last few years drain-ing away.

"Nunik," she whispered, knowing the one word spoke for all the magic and wisdom of the ocean at her feet. In the gentle caress of the warm breeze she heard a sigh of relief and understood her axis had just shifted. Profoundly. She could not, would not go back to what she'd been doing. As she dived back into the water no doubt lingered that she had been away too long from the home of her heart, from the spirit that gave her strength. Now she just needed to find another way.

# Chapter 12

The following day she found a note from Dee among her for-
warded mail.

*Been wondering how you are doing. Needing some help with
harvesting and preparing for next season. Money's not much but
the company would be great. Let me know. Dee.*

Sometimes you just had to go with the flow. Kayla threw together
her scant belongings, and a day later she was on the road, knowing
her arrival on the doorstep was the reply Dee hoped for.

Kayla was barely out of the ute before Dee rushed from the
house, dancing her welcome. Right choice, Kayla thought as they
grabbed her bags and headed inside. Night was near, but she could
see trees and hills enough in the grey dusk to know that this would
be a good place to land for a while.

It had been a hot day and though she didn't drink often, Kayla
was grateful for the cold home-brewed cider Dee offered.

"Cheers." Dee clinked bottles, took a long swig, and then it all
came tumbling out. "You may have heard a snippet or two, but we
have much to celebrate here. It took about a week to empty that
ravine of those filthy drums. Once they'd analysed the samples

the government made a big deal about it, brought in trucks and diggers and took away as much contaminated soil as they could identify. But then almost as soon as they were done, it started to rain like it hadn't done for near on three years." Dee grinned with delight.

"I tell you, Kayla, it was like the wisdom of Gaia herself. I thought of you as I stood in the driveway with the rain washing over me all warm and soft like tears of gratitude. Then it really pelted down, sluicing the ground as if determined to wash away any last traces of poison. And mostly it has." Dee shook her head. "We were so lucky. Some of those drums were really nasty, but the leaks came from a water-soluble acid and after the flooding … well, already most of the browning-off we saw is sprouting again. It's taken a good couple of years to turn around. You know we can never thank you enough."

Kayla felt heat spread across her face. She wished she could accept such praise without squirming. She still felt a bit of a fraud, little more than a conduit for something far greater than herself. But she had also been practising expressing her gratitude to those who gave, and to the gift itself.

"Thanks Dee. But it wasn't just me. You guys did all the hard work after I left."

"Well, that may be so. But this was about much more than restoring our water. Speaking for myself, you restored hope that there can be healing in this world gone mad." Dee nodded. "It's true. I came back home and turned all that good into the ground. Now that labour of love has grown into a harvest too big to manage on my own." She clapped her hands, beaming her delight. "I couldn't think of anyone I wanted to share it with more, and here you are."

Dee's old farmhouse had been built when wooden boards were

used to line walls inside and out. Carefully constructed with tin plates between the stumps and framework to block the incursion of white ants, ninety-two years later its timber was as sound as the day it was sawn. Ten-foot ceilings and generous windows made even the smallest rooms spacious and light.

Kayla's room was at the back, with a view across the orchard. It was a combination of library and guest room, the tantalising musty scent of seasoned books greeting her at the doorway. As they made up the bed, Dee invited her to feast upon the wealth of words in this collection, a lifetime in the making. Though tired, Kayla had a selection of seven books on her bedside table before she slept.

Days slipped into weeks to the steady rhythm of early mornings, long days, deepening conversations and hours of reading into the night until Kayla's eyes could no longer focus. Books initiated dialogue, the ensuing discussion referring back to other reading.

Between them, these two determined women brought the harvest in. As the weather changed they bottled, baked, dried, stewed, stored, shared and sold a surprising variety of produce, leaving the larder and their pockets richer for the wealth of it.

Both were private women used to keeping their own counsel, mutually respectful of the other's silences. One morning, rising earlier than usual, Kayla found Dee cross-legged before a little shrine. She had noticed the items before but never asked. Dee's eyes opened before she could back out.

"Sorry," said Kayla.

"No need to be. I was nearly done anyway." Dee's eyes were soft, almost dreamy. "Sit with me if you like."

Kayla sat. Dee's face was radiant, smoothed as if someone had wiped away the wear of weather and age. Even the room seemed suffused with a stillness belied by the wind beyond the window. Kayla closed her eyes, slipping easily into a slow, steady breath.

This was familiar. She had learnt how to source an internal space, to retreat in times of need to the quiet place that lay beyond the reach of the external world. But she had always been alone, in a forest, by a river or an ocean.

Her body relaxed, settling onto the floor, responding of its own accord. Colours swirled behind her eyes till there was nothing but a rippling blue orb falling endlessly into itself. Time drifted, as did she, seduced into somewhere deep, still and serene. Then, with a sudden breath, she was back. She opened her eyes knowing that they would be as soft and dreamy as Dee's had been before.

Alert to the movement, Dee shared a complicit smile that spoke of the profound peace that for this moment held them both in its embrace.

Eventually she stretched out her legs, breaking the spell. "Breakfast then?" she asked. Kayla just nodded, wanting to hold to the silence.

With the kitchen facing eastward, they made eggs and tomatoes, toast and tea, lit by the long probing rays of early sun. Birds sang their praises, and hearing the bustling activity beyond the window, Kayla had to admit the concept of silence in the Australian bush was a bit of a misnomer. Here alone there were over two hundred visiting species.

"That was really good." Kayla pushed away her empty plate and leaned back in her chair so she could look right at Dee. "I've never done that before. Sit with someone else, that is."

"To meditate, you mean?"

"Well, yeah. I've never given it a name. Just learnt to go somewhere else, where nothing could reach in. But only alone, and in wild places when the weight … when things got too much." Kayla sipped her tea. "So, why do you meditate, Dee?"

"Why? To remember all that I am, I suppose." Dee nodded,

looking far into the distance. Then, pulling herself to her feet with a shake of her head, she added, "But for now that includes a hungry menagerie waiting for their breakfast." And she was gone.

It made Kayla smile. Sometimes Dee reminded her of a darting fish, full of busyness. And relationship. That was the word. It was one of the aspects of this woman she so admired. It was as though over the years Dee had woven invisible threads of relationship with every entity inhabiting every dusty, damaged corner of this arid tract of land, weaving a life of meaning and connection that nourished and embraced not only Dee but any who came within her realm.

The next time Kayla rose early enough to join Dee, she found her own cushion awaiting her. Though Dee lit incense and used ancient oils like Heena and Khus, Kayla had learnt that this was a personal search for the nature of her spiritual self, unrestrained by the tenets of any religious creed.

Here, on this cushion, on this little square of carpet, as night fled the light of the new day, all else fell away. There were no boundaries here, no rules or limitations. Sitting together with Dee was enhancing the depth and intensity. Kayla began to experience an immensity of presence that negated any concept of finite inner space.

"So what is it you believe in?" Kayla asked Dee one morning as they sat in the quiet serenity that came after.

"Used to be nothing. Now I could almost say everything." Dee laughed softly. "I can no longer say that any one thing is more or less sacred, or has more or less intrinsic worth, than any other.

"But now, if you are asking about a mysterious, immortal and all-seeing god, well it makes no sense to me that such a being could exist, yet never intervene with those who allow terrible things to happen on their watch." Dee shook her head as if to banish the thought.

"Me either, Dee," Kayla agreed. "I've been into churches and ashrams and even temples looking for something, for anything I could find in the spiritual realms that might help me make sense of my water dreaming. And found nothing. Though they are supposed to be sacred places it was always men ruling from the pulpits, as if by some god-given right. So I tried books, and can you believe, every single avatar in recorded history has been male, with the devotion of us women to be compliant and submissive. How are we supposed to relate to that?"

Dee chuckled. "Too true, my lovely. It's not likely that you'll ever see yourself in any of those great halls of power."

"Well, there's that too. And as for this endless squabbling over which imaginary god is more real – what a madness of men wanting more and more power and immortality. And what a great excuse for war and the excess and profits that come with it. From what I can see, religions based on worshipping a godlike being beyond human reach have created all these divisions of our modern world. But what you have here, Dee – this I want to know." Kayla grinned shyly at her friend. "I too want to be able to say everything … and mean it."

"So then, my dear Kayla, perhaps your question really is, what do I have faith in? And that is a different story. The older I become the more I find myself returning to the spirit of the young. To reclaiming the wonder to be had in simply trusting all that I see and smell, touch, feel and hear. As my relationship with the seasons and cycles of this land has grown and deepened, I've found faith that even my short existence is part of something bigger and more profound than my limited mind can conceive. Something that includes me in its cycle, like a leaf on a tree, or a pebble on a mountain. And without my presence for its mere blink of time, that something would be not quite complete."

In the quiet that followed, Kayla closed her eyes and breathed deeply. She'd been so hungry. So alone. As she drew breath again she could almost taste the calm nourishment of Dee's simple integrity.

"What I can say," Dee continued, "is that these last few years have given me a powerful faith in the underlying primordial intelligence of nature. I even have faith that she will heal from our wounding and that life will go on long after we humans are a faint memory of a passing species."

Kayla could feel Dee watching her. These weeks together had eased the heaviness in her heart, but she still had so many questions. She searched for the confidence to speak the despair that she'd carried for way too long.

"Well I'm struggling with that faith, Dee. I'm not sure anymore that we can stop this downhill slide we're on. Time after time I'm called, and I go. We find the problem, we tell the incompetent fools in charge, and nothing bloody changes. The forests are decimated, and the rivers …" Kayla flinched as if a visible wave of agony washed through her. "I don't need to tell you how it is. She's hurting, really hurting. All the filth of our greed and indulgence is bleeding back into the systems and down into the oceans. I'm not even sure we deserve to continue as a species." Kayla looked down, feeling the tightness in her throat. "The thing is, I just don't know where my place is any more."

"I wonder that any of us ever truly do. Perhaps that very idea is an illusion in itself." Dee's voice was soft, suggestive rather than judgemental. She waited, giving that thought its moment of truth before continuing. "I've often wondered about this human desire to define one's purpose. The incredible reality of life is that we are each as unique as our faces and fingerprints, yet we still feel that we have to justify our existence. The pressure to stand apart, to be exceptional, is very much a part of the slippery slide that has led humankind to see itself as separate and even superior to the very earth that sustains us."

"Yes, that's it, it's this separateness. And the bloody arrogance that comes with it." Kayla sighed. "Humans think they are so damn clever. Surely we weren't just put on this earth to use it up. It's as though we're forgetting how interwoven with every element we are; that it's the same water flowing in our bodies, the same air we breathe, the same stardust that seeded everything that has ever existed, living or otherwise. You know what, Dee, I'm tired of feeling so damn frustrated and angry, but the world's stopped caring – and I can't."

Kayla closed her eyes, wanting to recapture the quietude of a few minutes earlier. "I don't want to be fighter. It contradicts everything inside me. I can't keep banging up against things, bureaucracy, corporations or whoever. It all feels like straight lines in a world that needs spirals and swirls and ebbs and flows to thrive. I'm afraid that the more I confront this system, the more I'll become like them, cynical and sharp and relentless and … unforgiving."

There it was, spoken out loud for the first time. Feeling exposed, Kayla looked up and saw only compassion in Dee's warm brown eyes.

# Chapter 13

The next evening, they sat out on the deck as grey storm clouds gathered in the western sky. Dee cleared her throat and settled back in her chair. Kayla had learnt this was often a precursor to a story or something else on Dee's mind. She looked down, hiding her grin of anticipation. She had so hungered for the depth of broad and diverse thinking Dee offered.

"Seems to me," Dee began, "that from the moment we're born, the moment we're separated from that infinite ocean of possibility, every aspect of our reality is labelled and locked in. Race, gender, religion, sexual preference – they're all just a bunch of cultural beliefs shaped into social structures, formed by the limited views of those who came before us. Illusionary boundaries, built to control and confine our immensity. Society demands we conform, but there are many of us who never do – and some who break."

Unexpected emotion choked any response Kayla might have made. That was her! Fitting in by diminishing herself had never come easily, and she had come closer to breaking than she'd ever been willing to admit.

"There's so much more that unites us than sets us apart," Dee went on. "Highlighting our differences may have been the most effective tool of all time to create fear, to justify war, and gain status, power and wealth. And for those at the top, well, what better way to distract ordinary folk from the things that really matter?" Dee spoke slowly, forming thoughts into words with a clarity that told Kayla these were not new ideas. "This thing we call life wants nothing more than to wake us up and shake us loose from this numbing civilised complacency. If we're willing and open, experiences do come along that shift our perception and expand our consciousness. But only if we're up for it. And only if we're listening."

Thunder rumbled through the far hills. A sudden sultry wind, heavy with the heady scent of impending rain, swirled around them, teasing at their clothes and hair.

"Ah, the perfect segue." Dee laughed. "I don't know how she does it. I was about to ask, if you have ever wondered where the word 'spirit' comes from?"

Kayla shook her head. "I've never really thought about it."

"It originates from Latin, 'Spiritus', meaning breath or a gust of wind. It's also the origin of respiration. In most languages, including English, the words for spirit, breath and wind come from the same root source."

"Spirit is breath. Breath is wind. Wind is spirit. I like that," Kayla acknowledged. "I can almost see it."

"Thought you might." Dee settled back in her chair, and Kayla knew there was still more to come. "I wasn't always as you find me, Kayla. There were many years I thought I was as small and sad as the world that had me in its grasp. Life was just a nasty mess of addiction, neglect and abuse. Days passed when all I did was wander along the river's edge, pretty much hoping that I would simply slip in and it would all be over." Dee took a deep, slow breath.

"But it never happened, and one day I was sitting on a bench when this older woman, Ruth, came and sat next to me. We got to talking of ways of seeing the world that no one had put to me before. Of how to take a step back so I could see the tangled web I had created – and change it. And I know it's hard to imagine when you see me now, but I had no idea that this life is a precious, sacred journey we can make our own. That we can choose how we live it and what matters to us. Ruth changed my very under-standing of what it is to be alive and my gratitude to her … well, I only hope she knows that I could never say enough."

Dee looked up and they shared a smile. Kayla hoped Dee knew that she too felt gifted with such a blessing. Like so many women's tales, Dee's life story ached with pain that would never quite heal. Often Kayla felt too inexperienced to respond, but she had learnt that it wasn't really necessary. It was the telling, the sharing, but mostly the listening and acknowledging that mattered. Unique as they were, each told of courage and resilience, but more than anything, each spoke of the search for safe haven and the chance to live gentle, loving, appreciated lives. It seemed so little to ask, and yet what a journey it had been for Dee to find her way here.

Kayla could only hope for the same courage, but already, like a warmth in her belly, she could feel a kernel of excitement, of change. Something in Dee's words had planted a potent seed of possibility.

"There by that polluted river, Ruth insisted I feel the wonder she saw all around," Dee continued. "Breath by breath, day by day, with the patience of a mountain, she reminded me of the touch of the invisible, urging me to feel the wind as it played with my hair, and the caress in the warming sun. 'Listen for the music of the air as it moves and, oh my, smell those scents,' she'd say.

"Then one day she drove us beyond the city's edge, deep into the bush – a new experience for me, I might add. There, together, we watched the dance of the earth's breath in the sensual sway of trees moving to the gentlest of breezes, in the seductive whisper of trembling leaves, and even the playful dance of wind on water." Dee's smile lifted with memory.

Kayla rocked where she sat as images swirled in her mind. Dee had her with the poetry, but it was the together thing that was really stirring her.

"We'd drive headlong into storms and wild weather, climbing hills to bear witness to the rush of rain-heavy clouds skating across the sky. We stood in raging wind and pelting rain till there was nothing but the dynamic presence of nature holding us. Till the day came that I could no longer doubt I was as much a part of this world as that rain, and the trees, and the wind and its breath was my breath. Till there was nothing I had to do to justify my existence other than to care for this entity that I'm a part of."

"Like her rivers are my veins." Kayla whispered.

"Yes, just like that." Dee nodded, and for a while they both just sat listening and watching as the spirit in the storm whirled and danced around them.

"It's a rare talent you have, Kayla. Not just the way you sense and interpret water, but how it becomes you, or rather you are becoming it. And how bravely you have worked to explore and grow, drawing on that watery well of inherent wisdom without mentor or guide. That's no small thing, my dear young friend, and I want you to know that I see you and love you for it."

Kayla shook her head, flushed by Dee's tribute.

"It's true. I feel like I'm the lucky one here." Dee chuckled. "Just being around your empathic way with all things water, shifts my being like an old, old memory. You live that connection in a way the rest of us can only yearn for. It reminds us of something deeply primal, something that maybe once upon a time we all knew. And it gives hope that one day we might get to remember it too."

"I would really like that." Kayla sighed with a longing of her own. Dee's words a glimmer of hope on what had been a long, lonely road.

"I've been thinking, dear Kayla, that if you could manage to put aside your highly developed sense of social responsibility ..." Dee stopped, waited till Kayla met her gaze. "Then perhaps the time has come to let others stand in the bonfires of political struggle."

"Could I really make that choice, Dee?" Kayla asked. "What if no one ...?"

"Someone will. It's not your job to carry the world, only to do what you can. We're not alone in this struggle. But, if we are truly changing the rulebook women have been raised to believe, then we are learning to choose nurture over sacrifice, and that means starting with ourselves." Dee climbed to her feet. "And with that thought, it's off to bed for me. I'm all done in, and tomorrow's already full. But please, let's have a fire soon."

Kayla stayed a while as the storm intensified, savouring the cooling touch of the wind on her skin. Lightning forked across the sky just before rolling thunder roared directly overhead. Her nostrils flared with the sweet tang of fresh ozone. The clouds opened and intense rain pounded on the old tin roof, as though insisting on her full attention. She stepped out into the deluge, savouring the spirit in the wind and the fierce pounding of the rain, saturating her senses, till there was no separation. She could do this. She would do this. She had all the wonder of this wild world deep within in. No, she *was* this wild world.

# Chapter 14

Once or twice a week since the weather had cooled, they had spent the evening out under the stars, contemplating the wisdom found deep in glowing embers and dancing flames. Kayla never failed to enjoy the simple satisfaction of gathering wood and creating fire. Over the years Dee had brought in several old logs, gradually honing them into smooth comfortable contours that, with a couple of cushions, offered all the ease and support a body could want.

Fading dusk came with a rare breath of moistened air, pungent with drifts of eucalyptus liberated by the day's heat. As was her habit Kayla needed no paper, only a match and a crush of dry leaves and twigs to start her fire. Wisps of smoke drifted her way, familiar and deeply comforting.

The flames had burnt down to a glowing nest of coals when Dee spoke. "I've been wanting to give you something, Kayla." She sat forward and poked the fire. "Something you can draw on in days to come."

"You already have." Kayla said. "So much more than you can imagine. Spending this time talking and working together … I knew I needed to get my hands in the dirt again. But sharing the harvest, and the retreat of your home – you must know that it has fed far more than my body." Kayla stopped, her throat suddenly tight with the intensity of feeling she had for this woman and her precious sanctuary. She searched the flames, seeking the words she really wanted Dee to hear. "You have grown me, Dee. You've stretched my thinking, my skills, but more than that, you've given me a pathway back to my internal quiet places, of spirit, and of peace. And I'm so grateful."

"Funny how us odd bods find each other," Dee said, and the smile they shared was as warming as the flames.

"But I don't know how to go back out there," Kayla admitted. "To leave this beautiful, gently woven life you've created. I don't believe the story any longer. I'm not sure that I ever did, but somehow I got swept in. Now I never want to play by their rules ever again."

"Then don't." Dee's response was so clear it cut through the air. She laughed and patted the cushion beside her. "Come, sit over here with me for a moment."

When Kayla sat, Dee reached for her hands, gave them a squeeze, then turned each one to hold palm upward in her own. "One day, these young hands, so warm and eager, will, just like mine, be etched with the story of the journey you choose to take. They will make manifest your intentions, your passions, and your dreams, all the time translating the spirit, the life force, or whatever you call it, of you – this most precious being we know as Kayla – into the physical realm of existence. Do you remember how it felt when you first reached for Ed's dowsing rods all those years ago?"

"I can. I remember everything." Kayla shut her eyes as the memory warmed in her hands before spreading as a rush of tingling joy into her body, as present as that very first time. When Dee chuckled and squeezed her hands, Kayla knew that she had felt it too.

"That was …ecstatic." Dee spoke softly, but there was no hiding the excitement in her voice.

"So you did feel it. I never knew that could happen." Suddenly a little shy, Kayla let go of Dee's hands and stood to poke at the fire. "It's hard to describe, but when I was young, I thought that it must be the way nature would feel if it could laugh. And sometimes I could even see it rippling through trees and across rivers and mountains. Like if ecstasy was energy, it would be connected and wild, and full and empty all at once."

Dee chuckled again. "This is the mystifying gift of you, Kayla. Experiencing your relationship wakes us up, shakes us loose. I can no longer think of it as a choice, but a responsibility for you to honour this gift, to embrace the wildly ecstatic, eccentric mixture of biology, intelligence and heart you've been blessed with."

"Easy for you to say. It's like I am *it*, but I don't know what *it* is."

"Then go back to your nan. Explore your roots. From what you've told me, she was a woman of water, and of the wild places that link you to remote islands and ancient stories. How did she learn what she gifted to you? What of the women who came before her, the long line that has brought you here, at this time, with this inborn connection? Aren't you curious?"

"Mum said they were all dead."

"Well maybe they are, and maybe they aren't. If you don't look you'll never know. I can't help but think the answers you are seeking lie deep in the past. If you learn more you might find ways that others could experience the empathy that permeates your being, to share what the world looks like through your watery lens. This is what you bring to every life you touch." Dee stopped and waited for Kayla to look up at her. When she did, Dee added softly, "I have absolute faith that you can do this, Kayla, whatever it turns out to be. Just please drop me a note, or swing by every now and again."

"I will," Kayla promised.

# Chapter 15

Ed's call came late on the following Friday. "I've had a bit of a turn," he whispered. "And I want to go home."

Calling the hospital back, Kayla learnt that Ed had suffered a massive heart attack. Luckily, he'd been visiting a friend in Patchewollock who'd called for help quickly. But the damage was extensive and so severe that only a tough old coot such as Ed could have survived. And time was short.

In less than twenty minutes Kayla was on the road. Nearly fourteen hours later she flew through the doors of the bush nursing hospital. *Please, please, please,* she was chanting to herself, the same refrain that had begun hundreds of kilometres ago. The nurse's nodding smile told her she had made it in time.

He didn't look like Ed. Deathly pale skin pulled over stark bones. But his familiar blue eyes glistened with gratitude as he recognised her. Kayla reached in among all the tubes and wires, claiming the hug she had travelled so far for.

"You took your time, girl." Ed pressed her hand. "Get me out of here, will ya? Please, Kayla."

"Course I will. Let me just go and talk to someone."

Against all medical advice, Kayla had him bundled in blankets and on the way home before lunch. Ed slept most of the sixty kilometres home, but she woke him as they came down his road. Turning into the driveway, Kayla stopped suddenly. As the cloud of fine bulldust that had followed them home settled around the car, they just sat a few minutes, gazing up to the house and vast blue sky beyond, watching the dancing heat lift from the roof and paddocks. Memories and emotions charged the air they shared. Both aware that this was probably the last time they would come home together.

Ed cleared his throat. "I'm not sad, you know."

"Well I am. What am I going to do without you?" Kayla made no attempt to keep the emotion from her voice.

"I got an idea. Let's see if I can make it inside."

Kayla was glad for her strength, as he had none. Always lean, there was little left of the man she had known other than the determined spirit that shone from his eyes. She propped him in a cosy nest of pillows and rugs where he could gaze across his favourite view. Two old eucalypts framed each side of the glass, an honour guard for their steward of a lifetime. When she opened the window the light breeze carried the whispering welcome of the leaves.

Ed would have nothing to do with Kayla's suggestion of sleep, insisting she make tea and join him. Unbidden, tears ran down her cheeks as she stood waiting for the kettle. Stubborn old bastard. What was he thinking, leaving hospital? But she knew why he had to come home. She would want the same, but at the very same time she wished him back into care that might give him days, perhaps even weeks or months that here, without the tools of modern medicine, she couldn't.

Kayla swiped at the tears. She wasn't really angry. Ed was old, and dying, and it was hurting like hell. She had never allowed herself to contemplate how much she would miss him. But this was the real deal. *When death stares you in the face there is no place to flee*, Dee had told her, gripping her hands with fierce intent on the doorstep before she left. *All you can do is let the grief and sorrow tell you of the love that never dies.* Kayla laid a tray and headed back to his side.

"It's all there, in my will." Ed indicated the top bureau drawer with a lift of his chin. Reluctant, Kayla dragged herself over and passed the document back to him.

"No, it's for you," he insisted, refusing to take it.

"I don't want it yet. I'll deal with all that when you're gone."

"You'll deal with it now, Kayla. While I'm still bloody here to talk about it."

There was resolve in his voice she couldn't refuse. Obediently she sat and withdrew the papers from the envelope in her hand.

"Now read the letter," he said. "Then we can talk."

She was halfway through when her eyes overflowed with tears she couldn't stop, for a grief she doubted would ever heal. When Kayla looked up Ed had closed his eyes. She let the letter fall to the floor.

"I heard that. Just resting my eyes, you know." His voice was as thin as the translucent skin that had taken over his body.

"I know," Kayla whispered back, stroking his hand. "Shh. We can talk later."

Ed's hand tightened. "Tell me you understand."

Kayla swallowed hard. He'd always shown her where courage lay, and for the first time, he was asking her to be brave for him. To stand at his side as life's final challenge took him from this world, from this consciousness, into whatever filled the spaces in between.

"I'm trying. So you want me to have all this, but not stay."

"It's what I always loved about you, fierce little hard-nut that you are." A smile barely lifted the sides of his mouth, but she knew.

"But I can't let you sacrifice yourself for the memory of what we've shared. You'll always have that. But this place is not for you. It was my dream. You must make your own." With that Ed coughed, and running out of breath he waved her away. "Sleep now."

Kayla tucked him in, smoothing an errant wisp of fine white hair back from his face. As if relieved of some burden Ed fell into a deep sleep, his breath quiet and steady.

She retrieved the letter and read it again. His intention was perfectly clear. He was leaving her everything, the complete unadulterated evidence of his life. But she was to sell every bit of it, except a few treasures she might want to keep, within six months after his death.

Ed had written of how he had heard her speak of her Nan, of the connection older and deeper than the simple love of family. He had listened carefully when Kayla had shared her dreams, and he had experienced first-hand her elemental relationship with water. So the gift he wanted to give was to enable her to go back to those roots. To return to the country of her grandmother's people, the one that resembled the lacework of land and lakes of her dreaming.

To validate his will, she must agree to travel to Newfoundland. And not just for a flying visit. To honour his legacy she was to find a way to stay till she learnt the language of her ancestral land, the way she had with him in his country, the way he trusted would bring her answers to her lifelong questions. After that she could do as she pleased with anything that was left.

Her heart was bursting. How could she possibly love him more than she did at this moment? He had seen into her, had recognised and honoured parts of her nature she was still learning to define. All he had ever wanted for her was to be everything she could. And with this gift – excitement was buzzing in the core of her. With his death he would make possible something she'd barely dared dream about.

Kayla moved her chair even closer and leaned into him. "I understand," she whispered into the warmth of his failing body.

"Thought you might," she heard in return.

They had three days together before he let go. Kayla wept as she filled a bowl, letting her tears merge with the water she had collected from the spring. Their spring. The same water that had nourished their dreams. Now hers alone. With great tenderness she washed Ed's lifeless body, preparing him for burial. How would she manage without him? Even so, she was grateful to be here. She really needed this last time together. Just to hold him, and let him go. Truth was, there could be no life for him once his heart had gone. She only hoped for the same dignity when her turn came.

The auction day was hard, watching all the treasure of Ed's life, things he had held and honed, trickle through the auctioneer's hands. But Ed's presence was so clear, so palpable, that when she booked her flights to Canada, she had to wonder if she should book two seats.

# Book Two

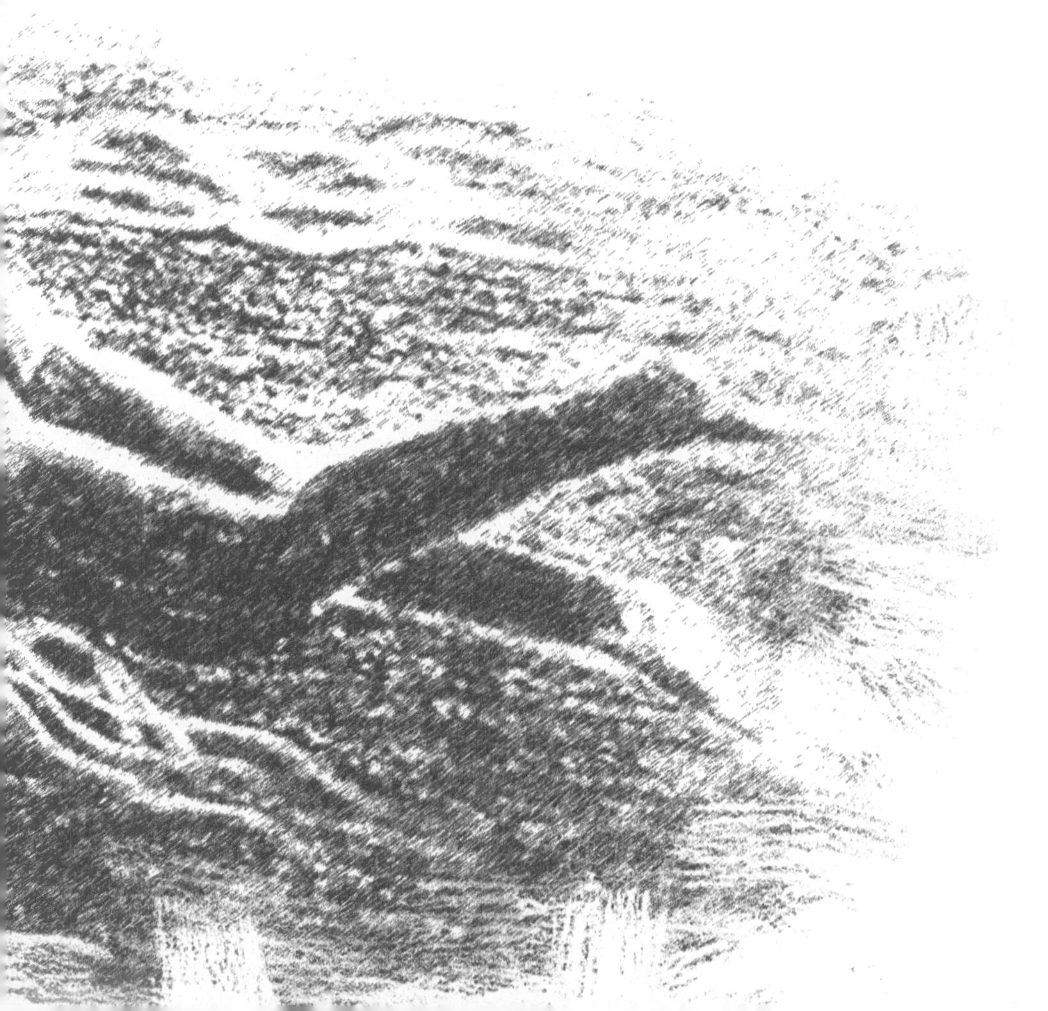

# Chapter 16

Blue-white light drew Kayla back from the strange worlds of dreaming into a new dawn. She lay sprawled across a lumpy old sofa, pretty much undisturbed since sleep had finally taken her in the lost hours after midnight. Beyond the window, beyond the pond, silhouette between water and sky, lay a thin strip of land. A perfect reflection on mirror-still water ran with the shoreline, fading as the early sun burned off the last shadows of night.

Working stiff muscles, Kayla came carefully to her feet, wary of the low ceilings of her new home. She could stand with barely inches to spare. That doorway would be deadly if she didn't stay alert. Kayla ducked under the lintel and headed outdoors to stretch fully into her long frame.

Those first breaths were intoxicating, the air rich with oxygen and ions, crisp and clear as the promise in the blue northern light. Moist tendrils of mist hung low, slung across the last pockets of yesterday. What a balm to lungs burdened with the ancient red dust of Australia. Ahh Ed, Kayla thought, taking a long slow breath on his behalf. What on earth have we done?

From the moment her plane had descended from the clouds towards the Avalon Peninsula, from that very first glimpse of the lace of green-cloaked rock that held together the innumerable ponds of Newfoundland, Kayla's heart had raced with recognition. Not only was this island the source of one strand of her ancestral line, but she was about to touch down amid the rocky realms of the dreaming that been hers as long as she could remember, dreams that had come like memories, though not her own, not from this lifetime anyway. She had come home to the landscape of her nights.

Ed had urged her to stay in Newfoundland for as long as it took to find her roots, to learn the ways of the land, and source the depth of her ancestry. And he was right. If she could find some way to stop long enough to feel the weather on her skin, unravel the memories borne on each breath, and listen till she remembered the woven melody of water, wind and wilderness she had first heard in the stories of her grandmother, she might just come to understand her innate links with this watery island.

Newfoundland. Kayla took a moment to appreciate the intention in the naming. Over the last few months she had extensively researched its history. For the last few centuries it had meant home and hearth to the fisher-folk who had made their lives here in hundreds of cliff-bound, rock-strewn, isolated outports. People brave enough to have taken on the hardship of this life rather than return home to the abject poverty of their class-driven status in England, or the potato blight of Ireland.

And they were only the newcomers. Though the winters were harsh, gentle summer days like this must have seemed like paradise for the Beothuk people who had roamed these woods long before Europeans even began to imagine their existence. She longed for the connectedness of tribal life. Though the extremes of the seasons would have severely tested her resolve, even those hardships appealed. Modern living was so soft and tame. How easily life could slip by without the markers of adversity to give it worth.

Before leaving home she had calculated that her antipodean home, the location on the earth's surface diametrically opposite to where she lived in Australia, was in the North Atlantic Ocean, with this island the nearest landfall. There was something delightfully symmetrical about being almost exactly half a world away from all that had come before. Twenty-five flying hours from Melbourne, via Los Angeles and Toronto, had brought her to St John's, the capital city of Newfoundland.

Kayla had spent the first day picking up a long list of necessities, having no real idea what she would find or really need. Hoping to have covered most contingencies, it was with a fully loaded rental car that she had finally hit the highway late morning.

Taking the Trans-Canada Highway across the isthmus from St John's to Gander had been a visual spectacle of rugged, craggy beauty. Talk about the land of her dreams! Rocks, lichens, and an infinite variety of forest greens surrounded a trail of blue-black water ponds. Every now and then an opening appeared with sweeping views of a minor fjord, others offered glimpses into hidden coves lined with the hardy houses of a small village. How tempting to turn into these villages with names such as Come By Chance, Little Heart's Ease and Happy Adventure. What a contrast to the misery of European colonialists' names for Australian locations such as Mt Disappointment, Foul Bay, Break-Me-Neck Hill and Dismal Swamp.

Her first impression yesterday was that she had come to the land of Christmas trees; snow-stunted native forests of predominantly spruce, birch and larch known locally as juniper, with an occasional fir and dogwood. The uniformity of the stunted conifers could not be more different from the erratic towering heights and irregularity of Australian eucalypts.

On her way here Kayla had dropped by to pick up the keys for the cabin from Thomas and Audrey, the owner-builders of her new home. All three so excited to be finally shaking hands on such an exchange. Over the past weeks they had spoken by phone across the world, negotiating the purchase and transfer of "Stranger's Gate", as the cabin had been named some thirty years ago. Pretty apt, Kayla had thought the first time she saw the ad, as it sent the hairs on her arms tingling. She still wondered how much influence the name had had on her decision.

Then there was the audacity of buying such a place "sight unseen". She had never been overseas before, and now here she was, sitting on the deck of her own remote cabin on a Maritime island of rock and water, lichen and conifers.

Thomas had taken one look at the hire car and shaken his head. "You will never be getting to the pond in that little thing." Before Kayla had time to worry or refuse, he had added, "It's our spare truck you'll be using instead, and I will not be taking no for an answer. If we needs it we can come and get it."

Thomas looked to Audrey for her nodding approval. "Come then, Kayla. Let's get your gear changed over and return the car. You'll not be paying for this one to sit on the side of the pond for no good reason."

With so much information and so many stories to share, it was hard to leave their warm and welcoming home. Later than planned, Kayla carefully crawled the borrowed truck over the last eight kilometres of rutted and rocky track from the bitumen to the pond's edge. She was deeply grateful for their inherent generosity, having needed all the clearance Tom's sturdy truck offered.

The fourteen-foot dinghy that came with the purchase of the

cabin lay moored to a rough timber wharf. Kayla transferred the supplies onboard, sorted the motor and, in a strangely surreal moment in time, chugged across the water, leaving the truck, and all that had come before, behind on the far shore.

Following Tom's map, she had made her way upriver through the first of a series of ponds towards the cabin. No longer was this place just a dream or a photo on the fridge. She was really here! With the last of the sun's light, Kayla pulled the boat alongside the jetty at Stranger's Gate.

She fired up the propane gas stove for a morning cuppa. Even such a familiar task failed to shift the trance of unreality. The sun was already climbing into the sky. Tempting as it was to jump into the boat and begin exploring the string of ponds along the river, there was all the unpacking to do, and she hadn't even explored the cabin yet.

But that could wait. Mug in hand, Kayla made her way out onto the deck, just needing to sit with the day a while.

When asked which side of the cabin the sun rose from, Audrey's reply had come from the poetry of this land and its people. "The sun rises to the right and sets to the left and what is between is to be enjoyed by all." How could she ever have resisted such an invitation?

Kayla's original imaginings of this journey included a few weeks exploring this island roughly one and a half times the size of Tasmania. But after she found Thomas and Audrey's advertisement, an idea had grown with an energy all its own. Purchasing a cabin offered the chance for a much longer stay, and even return visits. More importantly, it gave her access to wilderness that was near impossible to rent, let alone explore freely without company or guides.

Sometimes, Kayla knew, a step forward opens doors, offering glimpses of other ways, other worlds, other opportunities that can all too easily slide away before the courage can be found. Not this time. Not this damn time. Ed's offer had touched something so embedded in her cells, so deeply rooted in everything that connected her to the elemental world, that Kayla couldn't help but reach out with both hands and push the door wide. Now, unbelievably, here she was, alone on a pond, returning through Stranger's Gate to the land of her ancestors. Well, if this was the outcome, may the madness always run in her veins.

As if in response, the powerful silver body of a wild Atlantic salmon leapt from the water, flashing in the sunlight. Minutes later another and then another flew out, clearing the surface by more than half a metre, flexing their muscular forms in unbridled exuberance. Even though she had been told a salmon-spawning river ran directly past her cabin, she had never truly grasped what that meant. As if choreographed, several fins broke the surface just as another splash caught her eye, then another glimpse of a long sleek glistening body before it fell back into the deep. Each leap was a thrill, each time she couldn't help but laugh with the irresistible wonder of this world she had stumbled into.

There was clearly only one thing to do. Kayla stripped off her shirt, wriggled out of her pants, sprinted the ten long strides to the end of the jetty, and plunged in. For a dizzying moment her sense of reality shifted sideways as she plummeted from the sundrenched world into the realms of her dreaming.

She knew this water, knew the shock of its cold embrace, followed by the solace of its silken, smooth caress, and even the sharp taste of brown tannin, infused into the river as it flowed from the rivulets and springs and ponds upstream. Oh, how tempting to take that waterborne dream-breath so familiar and comforting. She surfaced instead, unable to resist creating whoops of delight that spread outward with the ripples and returned in resonant echoes, filling her ears with joy of her own making.

Kayla glided in and out till her muscles were warmed and awake, till the temperature of her skin matched that of the water, till every pore was ripe with moisture. Afterwards she lay on the jetty's worn wood, the warmth and wind drying her body.

Perhaps it was the gentle merging of the Maritime sun with the lulling company of water washing over rocks, but Kayla could not keep her eyes open. Surrendering to an overwhelming lassitude, in a moment she was floating in that undefined void between sleep and wakefulness. The sharp scent of spruce wafted on the breeze. Somewhere out there she heard an unfamiliar bird call, a repetitive song that gradually faded into the background along with any lingering awareness of her body as it lay on the hard wooden surface of the jetty. And still she floated, carried by something she could neither touch nor see, peaceful and wordless, just a vague thought that all was exactly as it was meant to be.

And then there she was. Kayla felt her mouth silently form the name she had come to treasure. *Nunik.* It had been months since she had appeared, yet it was as though no time had passed or mattered. Nunik cackled and rocked with a whole-body joy as if all her wishes had come at once. Even in that hazy dreamlike way, Kayla was aware of how she had longed for her presence, for this internal affirmation that cleared any lingering doubts that her dream travels with Nunik had been a fundamental part of the craziness that had drawn her on. Not just to Newfoundland because that was in her blood, but to Stranger's Gate itself, for this chance to saturate in this wild, watery wonderland. Nunik nodded enthusiastically as if she caught and concurred with that thought. And then was gone.

Slowly Kayla returned to the corporeal world of flesh and wood, of water and gently moving air. She felt that familiar longing to share words with her unworldly companion, and let it go. She'd had the nod. Right time, right place, right action, come what may. Time to get on with the real thing. She had a whole new world to explore.

# Chapter 17

Kayla sat up to survey her new surrounds. The shoreline ran several hundred metres to either side, dipping in and out of several coves till it disappeared around distant bends. Rocks lined the shore with the neatness of a deliberately built wall. Hard to believe that they must have been pushed up by the movement of the ice as the pond had frozen and thawed, year after year. Looking across the sunlit water it was near impossible to imagine the deep cold of winter. Tom had called this a pond. It must take a mighty large body of water here on Newfoundland to be called a lake.

Preparing for her journey, Kayla had read that Canadian waterways, lakes and rivers held a fifth of the world's fresh water. And that the glacier that had covered Newfoundland slid off barely ten thousand years ago, leaving about eight per cent of the surface as ponds, lakes and rivers.

Still feeling an edge of disbelief, Kayla made her way back inside. How strange it was to be standing in the three-dimensional version of the photo she had kept on her fridge since first coming across it in Newfoundland's Kijiji classifieds. Stranger's Gate. What a great name. Boarding that plane felt like stepping into a storybook of her own making. How many times would she get to do that in a lifetime?

Measuring ten metres by five, the cabin was all the room she would need for the next couple of months. A combined kitchen and living area looked out over the pond, with a good-sized wood heater right in the middle. Along the back were two small bedrooms separated by a bathroom of just toilet and sink. No running water meant there were no pipes to freeze and burst in winter. It also meant she would be carting any water she needed. The pond water was tannin brown but clean and drinkable. Just to be sure to avoid any trace of animal bacteria, Thomas had dug a well deep into the rock.

Taking a bucket, Kayla headed out to the unmarked paling shed that protected the well, little more than a metre squared and two metres high. Once within its walls she lifted the wooden lid. Moist, musty air rose to fill her senses.

Her hands trembled with unexpected reverence as she lowered the dipping bucket for the first time. As if taking part in an ancient ritual, she grasped the rope one hand at a time and drew the vessel back to the light. From a cupped hand she sipped water as cold and clear as liquid crystal, rock-filtered yet rounded with memory of the deep and dark, of earth and stone, telling of life underground far beyond the kiss of day.

Kayla closed her eyes, letting the water infuse her with a profound, permeating peace. Saturating her with a remembering that she was, and always would be, connected by this experience to a life that moves in its own time, slowly without pressure or haste or anxiety, as slowly and as eternally as mountains breathe and stars crumble.

She sipped again, and then again, each time with devotion, acknowledgement and gratitude for all the ways life had brought her here to this place, to this experience she would hold close for the rest of her days. Her well. Her home. Her story.

Once she understood the cabin's remoteness, Kayla had been determined not to return to any form of civilisation for at least several weeks. If she could be immersed, somehow merge with this exotic elemental world so dominated by water, just maybe she would come to know the source of the deep pull that had called her halfway across the world. It was happening already.

Back inside, Kayla reached for her fly rod. Frayed and worn with nearly seventy years of use and devotion, it was Kayla's most treasured belonging. For a long moment she stood just holding it, a warm rush of loving, treasured memories bringing joyous tears to her eyes.

"One day, maid," she said aloud to no one, and to everybody. She'd actually done it! By coming here to the woods and the waterways, Kayla had brought her Nan home. This was her grandmother's true country, not those parched dusty deserts of her adopted land. As Kayla gazed out over the exquisite blue water and the moist myriad of fertile greens, framed by the blue-white light of a northern sky, she knew with absolute certainty, that this was the very hunger that she'd felt in the old woman's soul.

One way or another Kayla had been destined to come to this island, drawn by a mystical thread of longing fostered by the guiding presence of her grandmother. Resonant in her whole being Kayla had heard the calling and responded. Today she had been visited by the essence of both Nan and Nunik, their tacit approval meaning more than she could express. Kayla unsheathed the beautifully crafted rod. Forget the unpacking, she was going fishing!

When Thomas had heard of her passion for fly-fishing, he had chosen a selection of handmade flies, both wet and dry, painstakingly crafted during the long days of winter. Kayla chose an orange one with a white tail to try first. As much as she was hanging out to take the boat further upriver, she decided to fish right off the little jetty. Time to test the waters, and anyway, she just really loved fishing. Catching dinner was only one reason. Really it was any excuse to be out with the wind, the water and the weather.

And as for the possibility of catching a salmon – well, what an extraordinary fish! After they had appeared in her dreams, Kayla had trawled the local library, hungry to know more. These Atlantic salmon were making their way back up the very same river in which they had been born. Each female full of eggs, ready to spawn and begin afresh the cycle of life all over again. Over winter they had swum to Greenland and back, a twenty-thousand-kilometre round trip. Unlike Pacific salmon, which spawned and died, many Atlantic salmon would make their way back to the ocean to do it all over again.

Her first strike came within minutes but was only a baby, little more than a parr, and too young to keep. A few more casts, and the temptation was too much for the local fish. Kayla landed her first decent trout, a good foot long and plenty for a meal. In no time she had another. As she cleaned her fish in the shallows of the shoreline, Kayla couldn't help but feel she had participated in this rite of survival many, many times before.

After lunch Kayla opened up her new home. Cupboards, boxes, tins of all descriptions and even the little generator shed were emptied and considered. What a collection of all the obscure odds and sods that life in a cabin in the middle of nowhere might require. During discussions Kayla had asked Audrey what "turnkey" meant, the phrase used to describe the inclusion of items that came with the sale.

"Everything is there waiting for you, cups in the cupboard, sheets on the bed. All you will need is your groceries and a smile," Audrey had replied with a grin.

And she was right. Stranger's Gate had come with everything to make a home, from the comfy sofa and beds to the full kitchen including a stove and fridge, a generator and battery system for lights and power, a marine and CB radio, a well of pure fresh water, even its own jetty and boat with a small but adequate two-horsepower motor included. More than that, Audrey and Thomas had left tools, ropes, a spare anchor, fishing paraphernalia, screws, nails and enough wire and string, as Ed would have said, to hold any outfit together.

As the sunset faded into a long twilight, Kayla tried to sit out on her bridge deck with a celebratory cider on Nan and Ed's behalf. Surely she had built up a tolerance for mozzies and bugs after her travels across her home continent, especially in the central deserts where flies outnumbered humans by millions to one. But that was nothing compared to the voracious black flies and nearly invisible midges that descended with the dusk. Two sips and Kayla was driven back indoors, quite prepared to take in the view through the window.

Somewhere there was a netting shirt that also covered her head and face that Audrey had encouraged her to buy, explaining that there were roughly only a hundred days of temperate weather here for these plants, insects and animals to complete their active breeding cycles. She would just have to get used to it. But not tonight. Tonight she would dine on simple fare from the safety of the screened windows of her new home. Home, eh? That word had rolled around quickly but it was true, she was settling in as fast as she had settled in anywhere.

# Chapter 18

The quiet was like a drug, the absolute tranquillity, combined with dense humid weather, utterly soporific. Kayla did little more than wake for meals and cast a line for long enough to land a couple of trout. Any attempt to read inevitably found her drifting back into dreamless sleep till hunger tugged at her consciousness. Each time she woke it was still there just beyond the glass; water as radiant and pristine as any she had known.

Perhaps it was weariness from days of travel, or from working six- and seven-day weeks right up to her departure, or perhaps just the relief of finally coming home to this land of her dreaming. But, by the third morning Kayla woke refreshed with the dawn, the malaise gone as completely as it had come.

A slight breeze sparkled the surface of the water lit with an early morning glow. It was mid July, and though the sun rose at about half past five, the sky had been wakening for an hour before that. Kayla wasn't sure if it was the intensity of the light or the underlying thrum of excitement at being here that had her up and at it with the earliest of birds. At home sparrows were feral, but here they were in their natural habitat. Already several different species were foraging in the early light.

Thomas's hand-drawn map showed the chain of ponds that

lay along Ragged Harbour River as it snaked inland towards its source. Though none could be seen from Stranger's Gate, eighteen cabins were scattered throughout the pond system. As far as Thomas knew they were all built and owned by locals like himself, most born and living in the coastal communities inhabiting the small coves and inlets between Frederickton and Musgrave Harbour.

During the exchange of maps, keys and information, Kayla had asked Audrey, "Why me?" Why, of all the people they could have sold their precious cabin to, had they chosen her?

Audrey shrugged and with that musical lilt as charming as the Newfoundlanders themselves, she'd replied, "I tink it were the accent."

After they had all laughed Kayla had asked again, "But seriously, why?"

It was Audrey who had answered. "Well, my dear, it was so unlikely that a young woman such as yourself would have found our advertisement in the first place. And then, for you to consider crossing the world all that way from Australia, just to come to our cabin in the woods. Well, we simply couldn't resist being part of your adventure, could we, Thomas? If you really wanted to do this, and it seemed you did, we could not stand in your way. And now here you are!" A shared joy rippled around the table, each touched by the magic of the astonishing turns that life can take, so gifted to those willing to risk the unknown.

"And why 'Stranger's Gate'?" Kayla wondered aloud. "Surely there must be a good story behind such a name."

Audrey and Thomas shared a smile of special memories before Thomas spoke. "It wasn't so much that we chose the name. It was more like we listened and it came. It's hard to describe, but whenever I stayed thereabouts it was as though I had left the world outside and arrived somewhere else. Audrey was the same, weren't you, my love?"

"That's right." Audrey nodded. "Despite all the years of fishing and camping on the ponds, it was like we were still visitors. The woods would grow back over the paths we trod, reclaiming flattened ground where we'd slept and the ash pits where we had made fire. Just as though we had never been. Not that I minded. But each time we were still strangers coming to a place we could but borrow for a time." Audrey paused, as if to find the words. "But this place was different. The very first night we stayed there together, right where the cabin now sits, we knew this was the site we'd been looking for." The smile she gave Tom was full of youth and memory. "As if we'd come home to where we belonged, to where we would always be welcome. Stranger's Gate became our favourite place in all the world."

"So, if I might ask, why are you selling it now?"

Thomas looked down, took a deep breath and went to speak but couldn't. Audrey took his hand. "Thomas has not been well, and we just need to lessen the load. Isn't that right, my dear?"

He nodded and looked right at Kayla, really wanting her to hear his words. "Just know that we couldn't be happier than for you to have it now, Kayla." Thomas cleared his throat. "Where's that map got to? I have so much yet to tell you, maid."

Now, with outboard fuelled up, life jacket on, anchor stowed, drinking water, knife, lunch, bug stuff, matches, hat and warm coat, Kayla was ready to go. She had a bit of a laugh at herself, feeling like a girl scout being so prepared, but truth was she was still a stranger in a strange land, and she really didn't know what was out there. Speaking of which, she better get that bear bell her friend Jamie had given her. It seemed small protection against a bear, but what would she know.

Last of all she packed her fly rod. The day before, Kayla had crimped the barbs on the flies she planned to use. Apparently, it was acceptable to use a normal hook and barb on the ponds, but once she entered the confines of the river only a single, barbless hook and fly was permitted. She liked the challenge of that, certainly seemed fairer, and wondered if she might make it a habit to shift that balance permanently more in favour of the fish.

After pushing off from the jetty, Kayla chugged the little motor along at the barest minimum. Signs were tacked on trees, reminders that she was entering a monitored scheduled river system. Thomas had been adamant that Kayla take notice. Should the fisheries find anyone with untagged fish or wrong equipment, all would be forfeited, everything to do with one's presence on the river including car, boat and even the cabin.

With map in hand, Kayla could identify swirling patterns in the water moving around some of the rocks she needed to avoid. She had marvelled at Thomas's memory as she'd watched him move his pen between the outlines of the river he'd drawn. Almost as if he were looking from the boat itself, he had marked the position of each hidden rock with a cross. Kayla made an exacting copy and sealed it into a plastic sleeve.

The air was cool on her face, the sun warm on her body as the boat followed the gentle turns of the river. Water levels were down from the spring melt peak, many of the hidden rocks starting to poke their heads above water. Budding water lilies and grasses were claiming whole patches of the surface where the shallows allowed. Though they were still closed, Kayla could see the yellow hearts of the lilies and imagined they would flower within days.

Beaten trails appeared out of the woods where moose, beaver and bear came down to drink.

It wasn't long before she saw her first beaver lodge, a chaotic structure of sticks of all sizes knitted together into a well-protected home. Suddenly aware of the noisy intrusion of the outboard, Kayla shut off the motor and drifted closer. How peaceful it was. After a while she stood up in the boat and, trying not to lose her balance, used an oar like a paddle to come closer still. But if there were any beavers inside, they weren't showing themselves. Perhaps it was the stories of her childhood or just the exoticness of the wildlife here, but there was something enchanting about the endeavour and artistry that had created this home of logs and sticks. Further along the shore she found a nice piece of beaver-bitten birch, a couple of feet long and at least four inches across, that had drifted free. Her first river treasure!

The current was gentle, the quiet too exquisite to intrude, so Kayla continued her way upstream using just the oars. It was a little awkward at first but less likely to startle the wildlife. And anyway, it was great to learn a new skill, especially a water one. She persevered with her technique till she had cut the splashing of her rowing action down to a minimum.

The river opened up into Stephen's Pond, just as drawn on Tom's map. The breeze was surprisingly strong across open water. Reluctantly Kayla fired up the outboard and motored slowly across.

Half a dozen cabins were scattered along the shoreline. Some, like her own, were almost right on the water's edge, others tucked further back into the woods. Canoes and kayaks were pulled up onshore or tucked in under cabins. What a great idea for her next visit. She grinned at the thought of a next time already forming in her mind.

Scraggy, rock-strewn islands were scattered throughout the

pond. It was hard to see just how many without circling each one, the shorelines blending one into the other. She passed tributary streams and what looked like another vast pond leading off to her left.

Newfoundland was just as it had seemed from above as she had flown in, so much water and so little land. It felt as though the very cells of her body were being moistened. A kilometre or so across the pond she found where the river continued, so again she cut the motor and paddled slowly into the opening.

A dead pine towered over the living trees. Audrey had told her that they were called starrigans, remnants of the forest that had burnt to the ground some sixty years earlier when a wildfire had levelled the whole of the Kittiwake peninsula over a devastating few weeks. A fire so hot, the locals said it had changed the nature of the rock below. The heat so intense that the coastal communities like Musgrave Harbour had been evacuated to Fogo Island, well off the coast, for the duration.

Re-growth had been slow, determined by the short summers and long bitter winters. But the birds, especially the raptors, loved the safety of the dead trees and for a while she had the company of a sea eagle as it followed her passage up the river.

Finally, she reached the turning point for the day where a small run of rapids linked the river to another pond. Kayla pulled the boat into the shore to have lunch.

On her way out from St John's, she had stopped in Gander to secure her trout and salmon licences. Newfoundland had chosen to monitor and safeguard their natural bounty of Atlantic salmon, and she was more than happy to respect the rules.

Locals and international visitors alike were only allowed a catch of six salmon a year. They were to be tagged through the mouth and gills, with day and month recorded, immediately upon capture.

Every river and tributary in the province had been graded according to whether it was, first, a scheduled salmon river and second, if so, into three classes. This depended on several factors including the salmon population, the size and remoteness of the river, how often they were fished and by how many, and by the habits of the spawning salmon themselves.

It was only after buying the cabin that Kayla had learnt that Stranger's Gate was on a highly valued, scheduled salmon river. Ragged Harbour River and all its tributaries came under a Class 3 rating, which meant that only two salmon a year could be retained from here by any one angler.

Tom had suggested the wet fly for this kind of water, so after eating her sandwiches she stepped out onto the rocks. Anywhere below the waterline was slimy and slippery, but there were just enough dry surfaces to keep balance.

Though she had caught many a trout on the fly, Kayla had never fished for Atlantic salmon. What an experience. It wasn't long before Kayla got her first rise that day, but the salmon weren't keen to take the fly and she really didn't mind. Even as she played the line out again and again there was a part of her that would be happy to never catch one of these swollen females, their bellies rounded with eggs. She would be quite content to wait to for the influx of males, the jacks, who would arrive later to fertilise the eggs.

But it was a whole new learning. These salmon ate nothing from the time they left the ocean to the time they returned, no matter how long that took. So, unlike a worm on a hook, or a hungry trout's interest in a fly, this was truly the art of temptation or absolute annoyance, depending on your view. The skill was to irritate the salmon with the fly until it snapped at it, then to snag it on the hook. And that was only the first part. The same strength and determination that saw so many salmon make it back up these rivers and tributaries more than once, also made it a feisty fish to land, desperate to run out your line in a last dash for freedom, snapping it off or slipping the hook to be gone in an instant.

Perhaps it was a deep compassionate reluctance to take such a life, but despite several rises and one late escapee, Kayla was glad she landed no salmon. It felt really good to have re-honed her fly-rod skills. And what a great excuse to spend a couple of hours right in the heart of a stream of wild salmon. Her arm was tired and her body stiff as she clambered back over the rocks to the shore. Time to be heading back before the evening onslaught of midges, mozzies and various other biting bugs appeared.

Kayla pushed the boat out and turned its bow for home, letting the current determine the pace. She stopped and fished briefly on Stephen's Pond, taking a beautiful pink trout home for supper. There was only one unmarked rock she scraped on the way, so she considered she'd done pretty well for a novice. Rather than the previous, debilitating exhaustion, it was the sleep of a day well spent that took her not long after sunset.

# Chapter 19

Hungry for retreat and isolation, Kayla had at first felt somewhat shy of the occasional boat passing her cabin en route to further ponds. But Newfoundlanders are a friendly lot, so it hadn't taken long for most of her neighbours to pull up to the end of the jetty and bid her welcome.

Their humble attention and implicit acceptance of her presence here were touching. Curious and shy all at once, generally quietly spoken except when it came to expressing their passion for cabin life, most of her visitors wanted little more than a good yarn.

Once they could all get past the accent that is. There was often a gap of several seconds between exchanges as each took a moment to hear the common English. Even across this small island the dialects were a little different for each cove and village, indicative of the isolated and self-sufficient nature of life here for hundreds of years past.

Jan had been the first to tie up long enough to come inside for a cup of tea. Mother of seven, grandma to twelve, Jan was an energetic, warm and curious woman and they soon found much to talk about. Kayla was delighted by the ease with which she slipped into light-hearted banter – life had become so damn serious of late.

Jan shared stories of the early days of European settlement some four hundred years before, of fishing families who had clung to the sides of the barely hospitable shorelines of their newly found land. Despite inadequate payments for their fish catch, which kept families permanently indebted to fish merchants, these clusters grew until sustainable communities evolved. Big families living side by side, so close and interwoven that the welfare of one became the concern of all.

Known as "outports", these villages could only be reached by boat, as there were few inland roads. During the 1960s, as many as 250 of these hard-fought-for rural communities had been forcefully resettled into larger villages and towns with better access to work and services. Despite decades of unresolved grief, pressure was still on for the remainder to surrender to pragmatic government policy.

Jan had come from one such community of eighty families.

"So if you could use one word to describe how it felt to grow up in Sandy Cove, what would it be?" Kayla asked.

Jan thought for a bit. "Perhaps safe. Yes, I think safe would be the word."

Safe, Kayla thought, not a word she'd have ever come up with. "So why safe?"

"You got to understand there was no one else, my dear. If we couldn't rely on each other we might as well throw ourselves in the sea there and then." This came with a grin. "Everyone had a bit of a role in the things they were best at. But if they weren't about, well you just had to step up and do what you could. We were moved in 1962, and I never did want to leave. I was only twelve years old and loved me life, loved the wild seas and all the things we did. Never did much like the cold but it's cold everywhere."

"So you've never been tempted by city life?" Kayla asked.

"Oh no, maid. Too many people, and strangers at that. Took me a while to come to terms with the life in Harbour Breton, but gradually we did. There'd still be days aplenty I miss the cove. Now we have our cabin here on the pond instead. And don't get me wrong, they are all good folk, but it's not the same. But then nothing's the same is it? Things are changing all over before you barely got time to turn around." Kayla could only nod in agreement.

Sam was her other visitor. From the first chat shared at jetty's end, Kayla enjoyed every quiet moment spent with this gentle man. A sailor all his life, Sam was a man used to his own company, and to giving sparingly, and only when asked, of his thoughtful, considered counsel.

He was delighted by Kayla's enthusiasm for fly-fishing and picked her up one morning for a tour of the river and its tributaries. This became a regular thing, Sam revealing yet another of his favourite fishing haunts each trip. It wasn't so much in his words as in the shared silences that Kayla felt Sam acknowledge her growing connection to this strange wild land.

Sam's cabin on the pond was his most treasured place in all the world. And after nearly fifty years working away on boats and ships, one could say that he'd been around, more than most. With a world outside that always seemed to be racing headlong into the next best thing, always looking beyond the present place and time, Kayla found herself grateful and heartened to be among people who loved where they were and what they were doing with a deeply satisfying contentment.

Sam and Kayla had been considering life over a quiet rum when a snowshoe hare hopped out along the jetty. From where they sat at the kitchen window, they had a perfect view as the hare went right to the far end and looked out across the water as if seriously contemplating a swim.

"It's going to jump in!" Kayla exclaimed.

"No, it's never."

"It is, look." After returning to shore again, the hare rushed back down the jetty, took a last scan of the water, and leapt in.

"Well, I never been seeing that before," Sam muttered, shaking his head with disbelief.

It was then that they saw the mink halfway down the jetty, hot on the trail of the hare. After a brief, almost regretful look off the end of the jetty, this bold mink suddenly lifted its head towards Sam's boat, catching the irresistible aroma of freshly caught trout. In the space of a heartbeat, the mink was slinking down the rope that moored the boat to the jetty and Sam was up and racing out the door to save his supper. After shooing the mink off the jetty and a farewell wave, Sam headed for home. Wisely, the hare made its escape, coming to shore some distance away, the swim no doubt reducing the trail of scent it would leave on land.

The interaction kept coming back into Kayla's mind – such an unusual play of nature. The first time she had seen a mink it had appeared as a liquid shadow, black as obsidian, melting through the rocks of the shoreline. Only as it lifted its head had she recognised the ferrety snout. Though feral to the island, mink had spread throughout Newfoundland after the collapse of several fur farming ventures.

The mink was clearly the dominant predator here. Confident and unthreatened, it had openly stalked its prey onto the jetty and then turned its intent towards the trout in Sam's boat without any fear.

In contrast, the hare had been watchful and uncertain with

every hop. In the end, with no apparent alternative, it had leapt into the unknown, doing whatever was needed to survive.

She'd sometimes felt like the snowshoe hare herself, pursued by a single-minded corporate predator. Always trying to befuddle and confuse, constantly looking for a new tactic. Yet the hare had survived its ordeal, making its way back to land to begin again. Perhaps this leap into the unknown waterways of Newfoundland, into this hidden sanctuary of wilderness still undiscovered by the insatiable masses, was her hope for renewal.

# Chapter 20

Blessed with a run of warm and balmy days, Kayla was seduced by a lingering interlude of light winds and mirror ponds. Saturated sunsets became long twilights dense with colour. Yet Newfoundland, this island of rock set off the eastern seaboard of Labrador and Quebec, was anything but predictable. It was a land at the mercy of weather and winds generated from the plains of mainland Canada to the west, the Arctic Circle to the north and the Atlantic Ocean to the east, and even occasionally reached by hurricane winds blown all the way from the Gulf of Mexico.

Among the rocks hidden between the countless layers of fallen spruce and birch that surrounded the cabin, Kayla found a bed of moss and lichen so soft that she took a book and relaxed back into its earthy green embrace. It had been months since she'd taken the time to read a full novel. Under the warm sun she managed nearly seventy pages before closing her eyes and drifting off to the music of water and birdsong.

A drop in temperature caressed her cheek, bringing her awake. Herringbone clouds had appeared high in the clear blue sky, heralding lofty winds and changing weather. She watched them drift, still lulled into a sense of complacency. Wind began to ruffle the surface of the pond in erratic patterns, dancing over the water as if not quite sure where to land. Then suddenly, there was a deeper chill in the wind that shivered across the sun-kissed skin of Kayla's arms.

Ominous clouds built above the western horizon in ever darkening layers of impending weather.

The temperature dropped further. As if to drive the message home, the cabin door slammed with a resounding thud. "Alright, I hear you!" Kayla said to no one in particular, and went to retie the boat, lifting the outboard motor clear of the water, just to be sure.

Waves appeared as the pond took on the energy of the wind. Yet when the rain came, it was far gentler than she expected. Sudden summer storms in Australia often arrived with drops that hit the hot pavements of the city, or the thirsty sands of the desert, with wet splotches the size of a hand, or with hail as hard and large as golf balls. But this rain was soft and small and cooling, as if it couldn't make up its mind as to whether it was mist or rain. Kayla sat out with it for as long as she could but there was a definite chill in the driving wind. Reluctantly she headed inside and, after changing out of her damp shirt, took up a chair before the window to just watch the weather pass on by.

The pond turned from blue to grey as though the black of the water offered no colour of its own, reflecting only that which was given from the changing sky. Rain played on the roof and across the water with a steady rhythm that never let up all that day and the next. It wasn't so much a torrential downpour, more like someone had flicked a switch, turning the dense humidity of the previous day into a solid form.

Days drifted into nights, sun into rain and back again. Sometimes Kayla wondered how to justify this time of retreat. An odd cabin dweller dropped by here and there, introducing themselves, curious about this Australian woman alone here on the ponds. No one troubled her for days on end as she simply rested, renewed and restored the equilibrium that had come so close to burning out.

It had always been hard not to feel more like a witness than a participant in the world around her as it hurtled headlong into a future of consumption and self-interest. Nan had taught her how to flee the noise and chaos and pressures of the cities for the quiet places. Places where she could think her own thoughts. And she'd really done it this time. Just when she needed it most.

People sometimes reacted to her tall, strong presence as if somehow threatened. Add that to her fey and independent ways and it was no surprise that she'd felt that step apart. The irony was that it was the very breadth of her passions and abilities that had enabled her to be here like this, alone in the wilderness.

And now here she was, sitting on the deck of a cabin in the wilds of remote Newfoundland. Never more present. Never more at home. "Yes, maid," she called aloud, to the trees, to the river and the pond, to the wild and exotic animals of this watery realm. Thanks, Nan.

She stood and stretched into the sky, savouring this fullness of being, the strength in her body, the reach of her arms. Oh, the liberty of solitude, free of being watched and judged, of the pressure to comply, obey and submit. How could she ever return?

All she knew for certain was that she could not, with any integrity, be anything other than this creature of nature so at home in the rivers and the woods. She'd never meant to be a contrary or diffi-cult child. Truth was, as with everybody, it was the accident of her genes, the time of her birth and her essential nature that defined the struggle. All she ever wanted was to live fully and love well.

It was only as she'd reached her twenties that she'd come to understand the sense of threat just being herself generated in such a role-based culture. It never made sense. What were they so afraid of? A strong, capable, thoughtful girl? It was just ludicrous. Ridiculous even. But being here and doing this, living this wild life, was finally truly honouring the gift of a body and spirit strong enough to survive almost anything that might come her way here on the pond. And beyond.

Could she have said yes without the skills she had learnt along the road to Stranger's Gate? Maybe. But maybe she couldn't have dreamed it up in the first place.

Suddenly she was thinking of home, swamped by all she had left behind. It had been bound to happen sometime. Ah Ed, what a gift you were. Kayla sat with the ache of him for a while, letting it gradually dissipate in intensity until he again slipped away into yesterday. This was exactly the right healing.

She would return to the fray soon enough but, for these couple of months, all she needed was to float on a pond somewhere far, far away where the water was clean and abundant.

Kayla landed and kept her first salmon, a jack, and spent the next three days eating it for lunch and dinners, not willing to waste a mouthful of the gift. She used the outboard to travel further upriver and floated back down with the current, rowed across ponds, explored numerous islands, and climbed along the banks of the tributaries. She watched beaver, otter and mink, osprey and eagle. She heard foxes, pipers and owls in the night and songbirds in the day, falling under the enchantment of the loons that frequented her pond, spellbound by their haunting call.

As if responding to her quiet presence a variety of birds returned, feeding boldly on the ripening berries of her wild garden. Occasionally she was joined by a snowshoe hare or a chatty, cheeky squirrel. She even found herself watched more than once by the smallest mice with the cutest ears she'd ever seen.

After seven weeks Kayla knew without doubt that she had passed through that gate. She had come from somewhere and arrived somewhere else. This place had always been in her blood. In communing with this fertile, vibrant landscape she was shedding some of the urgency of the ache that drove her. Unlike most of the world she dealt with out there, this land had a passive energy, an infinite patience, never demanding of her presence, willing to wait for all time till she was ready. Well, perhaps she nearly was.

# Chapter 21

Soft rain had returned, rarely seeming to fall with any force, yet each day raising the level of the pond by at least a centimetre or two. When the sun came out, the atmosphere changed rapidly from cool, saturated and heavy with mist and rain, to sultry and dense with heated moisture. When it became unbearably close inside the cabin, Kayla took to the river.

She had now travelled beyond the edges of Tom's map, taking to the oars more often than not as she explored unknown brooks and ponds. Noticing what appeared to be an old track leading into dark woods, she pulled the boat up onto the rocks and secured it to a strong sapling.

Kayla sat on the shore long enough to eat her lunch, thinking it might be safer not to have any scent of food drifting from her backpack. Tom had said there were only black bears here, smaller and more timid than their grizzly relatives. He'd also said she would be lucky to see one, as they were both rarely seen and more likely to fade into the woods than attack. Though she had been here for weeks, she had always stuck close to the water. This was her first foray inland and she was not quite sure what to expect.

It was hard to count the ways this land differed from her birthplace. One main bonus was no snakes. After a lifetime in Australia, trained to check every step when bushwalking or even just strolling in parklands, Kayla still had to remind herself not to study the ground or react to thin dark sticks.

But this place needed a different wariness. Despite the stumpy height of the woods, the track was dark and thicketed, full of shadows and shapes Kayla was yet to recognise and fully trust. She hadn't seen many animals yet, but they were there all right. They had almost certainly been quietly living alongside each other. Kayla frequently felt a sense of eyes upon her; a sense that, camouflaged by the shadows just beyond the cabin and along the riverside as she floated by, something, or someone, was watching. Was it instinct or anxiety? Was it animal, or something older, more primal, even mystical? The fact that she might never know was definitely part of the thrill.

Kayla was comfortable with her own company and abilities, but this would have been a good outing to share. Within forty steps the motley light had swallowed her up, and the river was out of view. Though previously cleared, this was not a dirt track. The only substance resembling dirt that Kayla could see was peat. Walking was a matter of determining what lay beneath the carpet of thick lichen, moss and miniature fungi that had created a deceptively flat surface. Every other step that wasn't a rock or a root was a tumble of rotting limbs and bodies of fallen spruce, remnants of those trees that had succumbed to the bitter winters, only to be subsumed by the ever-encroaching lichen.

There was something peculiar to conifer forests that Kayla had first felt in Australia. As she and her friends had searched pine plantations for edible fungi, they had often stumbled across the red-and-white toadstools with all the implied magic of Alice in Wonderland. The feeling was the same here only more intense, more exotic, more encompassing. In Australia the pines were spaced for log harvesting but here they closed ranks, barely a metre from the track becoming an impenetrable tangle of prickly interwoven limbs.

Distracted by the miniature worlds of wonder hidden among the lichen and moss, it took Kayla nearly an hour to reach the path's destination. The forest opened to a clearing and someone's dream cabin built deep within the woods.

It looked intact but untended. All the windows were boarded up and the windswept debris showed no one had been here for quite some time. As she got closer, she could see how the doors and window boards were peppered with dozens of outward-facing two-inch nails. Ouch! That had to be serious bear protection! Enough to stop any creature from pushing their way in. Kayla scanned the forest, listening into the silence, feeling a bit like the hare, only with no idea from whence the attack might come.

"Settle down," she muttered, but it had suddenly brought home the very real risk. These nails were serious protection against a powerful animal who, when threatened and driven to act, would be beyond terrifying. Kayla tried the handle and, finding it unlocked, slipped inside. She moved from window to window, scanning through the cracks, seeing nothing within the dense foliage. But her hackles were up and the strong sense that she was being watched was as present as it had ever been.

What was that? Something had moved in her peripheral vision just as she stepped back outside. As though only to be captured in a glance, it vanished as quickly as it came. But she knew this movement and the image that came with it. It had happened before, weeks ago in the woods near her cabin. She had disregarded it then as fanciful, even wishful thinking. But this second time? There was no doubt. Camouflaged but not hidden, the same face, same eyes catching hers, even as the same fleeting vision, barely discernible in the dappled forest light, faded back into shadows. A presence, and yet not …

Tribal. Ancient. Timeless. Breathing slowly, Kayla sat out on the steps, taking time for her body to disperse the adrenaline. Not so much afraid now, as deeply excited.

It had always been part of her intuitive understanding that, just as the cells of our bodies hold the memories of the powerful experiences of a human life, so too would the earth hold a memory of those who had been before. That the spirit energy of those with a deep relationship to country remained interwoven in all that had been.

In the emerging philosophy of quantum physics Kayla had found theories that asserted that time itself was not a line, not a steady progression of one event after the other. That all that had been, was and would be, coexisted across time and space, infinitely connected in ways that most modern human beings had lost the capacity to perceive.

This was what she had sought but barely dreamed possible, why she had created this retreat as the first part of her stay in Newfoundland. And why she had needed to saturate her whole being in a primal landscape before sourcing the trail of her bloodline. She had been seeking the connection that would leave no doubt that her roots ran through rivers far deeper than the surface settlement of the British colonisation of Australia.

Strong again on her feet, and emboldened, Kayla returned along the hewn track. Though she had forgotten the suggestion on her trek inland, she sang her way back to the boat, giving any lurking bear plenty of warning to fade back into the woods.

Kayla held no fear of the forest as she walked, her body thrilled and invigorated by the experience. But also it held an edge of sadness as she realised that this precious and rare time of solitude was coming to its natural close. Her communion had run its course. She felt rested, nourished and connected. It was time to find her family.

# Chapter 22

Kayla pointed the boat homeward and, with an occasional paddle and rare use of the motor, drifted downriver. There was one more thing she wanted to do and there wouldn't be a better time.

Martin's Point was a ninety-degree turn in the river forming a natural still-water lagoon, or billabong as she'd have called it at home. Beds of water grasses, reeds and lilies extended as far as their roots could reach. Each time Kayla had boated in here she'd caught a good-sized trout or two. Off to the right, Wilson's Brook joined the river. As one of the larger tributaries, it was a favoured salmon-spawning river. There was no fishing permitted at all once you entered the brook. But that wasn't why she was here today.

A few days ago, while idly gazing down into the water, she'd realised she was witnessing the fluid silvery blur of multiple layers of moving salmon. Within moments they had dissipated back into shadows. But they were there alright. She'd had no time to linger that day, as dark clouds were rolling in and she had needed to race the rapidly deteriorating weather back to the cabin.

But today she made her passage through the reeds and pulled the boat up to the shore. After finding her goggles, she slipped silently over the side of the boat and into the water. This lagoon had created a perfect habitat for the salmon to hide while waiting to leap upstream to spawn. Last time she was here, the shadow of the boat hadn't actually scared them away, so her plan was to just float across the surface with as little movement as possible.

Kayla had long ago honed her ability to stay under water, releasing her breath in gradual increments, till people on shore would wonder if she was ever coming back. With almost imperceptible movement, she used her hands and feet like flippers to propel her into the centre of the lagoon.

At first she saw only an occasional flash of silver. As the water deepened, she lost sight of the slime-laced plants that clung to the rocks lining the bottom. Slowly, with minimal movement, she lifted her head to the side, taking the breaths she needed. Then, between one moment and the next, as if she had become part of the pond, salmon appeared beneath her. Materialising out of the gloomy periphery, suddenly layer upon layer of sleek salmon swam below where Kayla hung suspended in the water.

As slowly as she could, Kayla lowered her hand to the full length of her arm and waited. Several breaths later, just as she turned her head back into the water, she felt a touch. After the first glancing contact the salmon circled and returned. Tentatively Kayla turned her palm up to form a rounded platform. She watched in awe as the salmon came into her hand and, for an exquisite fragment of time, nestled against her skin, allowing her to feel the power of its muscular body. A surge of energy pulsed through Kayla. Images rushed through her mind of brightly coloured, luminous maps. Continents lit by the arteries and veins of rivers and streams, by the pooled collectives of wetlands and swamps, and all the ways they drained back to the heart, to the oceans that drew them home.

Then as quickly and silently as they had come, the images were gone. And so were the salmon. Wishing for gills, as she had so many times, Kayla duck-dived to the bottom and pulled herself along the rocky floor. An occasional streak of silver caught her eye, but there was little to see other than a couple of old bottles and cans she took back to the surface.

What an experience! She knew without doubt she had touched into the source itself and could barely contain the ecstasy that surged through her body. And how would she ever stop smiling? Tears of joy burned her eyes. She sat in the boat a while till she could focus enough to turn the boat into current and float back downriver.

As she poled the boat through the rocks of Coady's Tickle, salmon leapt from the water in a dusk frenzy. No longer tempted to fish for her supper, Kayla celebrated the innate wisdom of nature that guided these salmon on a remarkable journey far into the North Atlantic and all the way back home to this rugged island to spawn. She found she had no hunger to break the cycle.

That night, for the first time, Kayla couldn't sleep. Or more correctly, stay asleep. Each time she started to slip away she'd wake startled, as if the adrenaline of the day had left traces in her veins. As the night became cooler, she lit the wood heater and sat with the door open dreaming into the flames. How could she ever leave this idyll she had found? But this sojourn was over. Whatever else Newfoundland had still to offer, she had work back home she couldn't leave undone.

It was so peaceful here, so pristine. Other than spring-water directly from the source, no flowing waters had ever been as pure and untainted as these. Never had she felt so cleansed and blessed by her affinity. No wonder the salmon found the strength to return year after year. And she would too.

There was no point going back to bed. She was far too ecstatic, buoyant even. She brought out a nest of blankets and settled down in reach of the gentle warmth.

The sound of crackling pine drew her out of oblivion. For a moment Kayla panicked – Oh no, the fire! But it was not the cabin that appeared around her. She was in a large cavern with shimmering trickles running down the dark walls. Through dancing flames she began to make out a face. Nunik!

In a far recess of her mind, Kayla understood that she was dreaming – in that realm that crosses between forms of consciousness. At that recognition Nunik beamed and nodded as if Kayla had just made some necessary transition. Nunik's body continued to materialise until she became the shiny sleek form of a full-bodied breasted seal, running with rivulets of salty water as if barely risen from the ocean's depths.

Kayla bowed her head in an expression of the reverence she felt. Nunik began to cackle in a way that took over her whole body. As Kayla looked up Nunik shook her head.

"You think too much, child."

It was the first time Nunik had spoken, and Kayla didn't know what to think.

"You are surprised I speak as a seal?"

Kayla nodded. "Is that who you are?"

Nunik laughed again. "I am whoever you need me to be. Today a speaking seal. Tomorrow, who knows?"

Kayla waited, tried not to think.

"But at last, you have come. I have something for you." After rummaging around in the folds of her abundant skin, Nunik reached her flipper through the flames. Wary of the fire, Kayla hesitated.

"Take it, Kayla," Nunik commanded. "You must no longer fear

what you think you see." Then the fire was gone and Kayla was leaning over a precipice that fell away into absolute darkness. Nunik was watching her from across the abyss, flipper still extended. Could she do this? Could she reach that far? It took all of her willpower as, holding to the merest illusion of balance, she stretched forward to accept the gift. As her hand touched the wet seal's skin, Nunik pulled back. Desperate, Kayla grabbed for a hold, but her fingers slid uselessly on the silky fur and she screamed as she fell down and down into blackest nothing. Then out of the blackness she heard her Nan speak. "Let go, maid. Trust the fall. Nothing is as it seems."

Suddenly the terror was gone, and she was back at the fire. This time, as she reached right into the flames, Nunik cackled and nodded and passed her a gift.

Kayla woke hot and sweaty, tangled in the nest of blankets. The cabin fire had died away, but the room was unnaturally hot. She closed her eyes. Her hand was still clenched shut. She opened it a finger at a time, but nothing was there. Yet she could have sworn she could still feel something. She closed her hand again, seeking memory of the dream. It was there all right. Her hand knew its shape.

Keeping the sense of its form intact inside her closed fist, Kayla found the pouch of earth and water treasures she had gathered since coming to Newfoundland. It held a collection of the gifts of nature that had touched her soul. Reverently she slid her hand inside and released whatever memory shape it contained. Maybe one day she would know its meaning, what her dreaming mind had failed to grasp. As Kayla put the pouch away, she wondered if it was the wind she heard, or the echo of Nunik's laughter.

# Chapter 23

The sound of the motor was dying away by the time Kayla made it to her feet. She had fallen back into a dreamless slumber, but now awake, was struggling to clear the unworldly images of the night. Jan was throwing a rope around the small bollard at jetty's end and, in the unspoken etiquette of the pond, would be awaiting Kayla's appearance before coming to land.

"Morning," Kayla called as she stepped from the doorway.

Jan looked up, her smile instantly reminding Kayla what she liked about this older island woman. "And morning to you. Not too early I hope?"

Kayla had no idea of the time, but a quick glance at the sun told her the day was well started. "Of course not. You coming in?"

"If you pop the kettle on, I've just got a couple of things," Jan replied, reaching down into the boat.

Kayla threw some cool well water on her face, hoping to clear a little of the mind fog, still straddled between the deep dreaming of the night and the new day.

Jan's full frame filled the doorway and as she entered the room it was with a presence so solid and grounded that without thought Kayla threw her arms around her. It was unexpected but not unwelcome, and Kayla's fierce hug was returned with a strength that told Kayla this woman enjoyed their connection just as much.

Jan sat at the table and Kayla turned to the kettle, both a little coy of the intimacy. Jan tabled a bag of fleshy white fish.

"I've brought you a bit of cod. And a nice piece of haddock too."

Kayla's mouth watered at the thought. These were generous slabs of the Maritime's most abundant ocean fish. "Thanks Jan. I will savour every succulent mouthful," she said, popping it straight into the fridge. "Your own catch, I presume?"

Jan nodded. "The whole family's been out for the last few days bringing in the quota. We've frozen what we can, and we'll have some salted for you to try soon. I'm hoping to be making you some brewis before you go."

"Brewis?"

"Yes, now that's an old island favourite. We soak hard bread, which you may call hard tack, and mix it with our salted cod. It's especially tasty scattered with scrunchions, crunchy little pieces of rendered salt pork fat." Jan laughed as she watched Kayla scrunch her nose with uncertainty. "It really is quite delicious."

Mmm, rendered salt pork fat. Kayla laughed. "Maybe I'll just take your word for it, for now."

She was acutely aware of her imminent departure and the way she would miss this unlikely friendship. "It might only be a few more days," she confessed quietly.

"I knows that, my sweet. That is also why I'm here." Jan pulled a notebook from another bag. "Now I understand that you're an independent and private sort of girl, and I hope you'll not be minding, but I had bit of a look into a couple of things we'd spoken of."

Intrigued, Kayla drew her chair closer.

"You did say your grandmother was born on Long Island, on Hermitage Bay? And the family name is Madec, right?"

Kayla nodded.

"Well, I've been thinking who did I know around Gaultois, where many from Piccarie were relocated to. My cousin Dorrie lives near there in Head of Bay d'Espoir, and she's not a woman to miss anything going on. Anyways, to cut a long story short, we think we've found your great-grandmother's sister."

Oh, how she had hoped for this. Never wanting it to be true, what her mother had said, that any direct relations of her Nan would have already passed from this life.

"My great-grandmother's sister would be my great-great-aunt. I didn't even know she existed. Mum was never interested, never wanted to talk about it. She said they were all dead anyway." Kayla shook her head. "She must be very old by now. Is she …? I don't even know her name."

"Annie Marie Harrison is her married name, but she was born Annie Marie Madec. Ninety-three years old, I hear, and still managing in her own home in Harbour Breton, though her late husband, Gordon Harrison, died about five years ago."

Jan referred to her notes. "But now it gets really interesting. Dorrie says there's an old tale about Annie's grandmother being taken off a Spanish pirate ship wrecked off the coast in 1882."

"Really? A Spanish pirate ship," Kayla mused aloud, trying to get a grip on what that might have meant in the late eighteen hundreds.

"But the story keeps on," Jan added. "This woman was recorded as being of unknown background, and was likely to have been captured and kept by the pirates for some time prior. Unfortunately for those poor women this was not an uncommon occurrence in those days."

"But unknown background?" Kayla repeated, this time a question. "What does that mean?"

"It's what they used to say of Indigenous folk when there'd be no written records. If she were from the south coast she might have been Mi'kmaq, or other First Nations peoples who had travelled north. Dorrie speculates that she were taken from the Inuit in the far north, but that you will have to confirm for yourself."

Kayla's mind raced with the implications. This woman was alive! And may have known her Nan. Other than her grandmother, Annie Marie Harrison would be the first relative on her mother's side she had ever met. "I don't know how to thank you, Jan. You can't begin to imagine what this means to me."

After making Kayla a second cup of tea, Jan sat back to the table. She gazed a long moment out the window, thinking carefully before she spoke. "I do have a notion as to what it means. My first husband, John Samuel, was taken from his family owing to his mixed heritage. After we were married John searched for his family, but his mother had passed and the damage done. They were no longer of each other's world. He didn't know how to go back, and all that was past kept him from moving forward. I don't believe he ever recovered from the grief. I … we lost him to an early grave just after he turned forty."

Jan's story was sobering. Both Canada and Australia had an ongoing history of mistreatment of the most vulnerable within their Indigenous cultures. Both had stolen children right out of their homes. Both countries had been asked for an apology and compensation, both had responded with empty hands and promises.

"I am so sorry." Kayla spoke into the silence.

"There's no need for that now. Though I do believe that if genetic tests were done on the majority of Canadians they might be a more than a little surprised at the results. But enough —" Jan stopped and smiled at Kayla. "Tell me now, maid, what will you be doing with all this exciting news then?"

"I'll go … go and meet my great-great-aunt Annie and have a chat I guess."

"Best kind." Jan agreed, coming to her feet. "Just keep in touch, girl. This has been really special to me, meeting you here and all. Perhaps you'll even come back to us one day?" It hung as a question.

"It'll be like I never left." Kayla grinned. The hug they shared lingered longer than the first, as if both were imprinting a memory to treasure. As Jan chugged away in her little tin dinghy, Kayla felt further regret to be leaving the pond, the cabin and all that it had come to mean to her in a few short weeks.

That afternoon Kayla packed. It had happened again, right on cue. Funny how just the day after she'd realised she was ready, at last, to follow the trail of her genetic line, Jan had come with this information. It was as if the very making of the decision manifested the life that came next.

It had been like this ever since she'd turned her attention to Newfoundland. Doors had opened. As if you just had to be willing to accept the quest, and life would steer you to the people who could help and show you the way. Kayla paused and looked out at the shimmering water. Just a couple more days on the pond, but then she must take this gift and explore the trail of its offering. Come what may.

Tom and Audrey insisted Kayla join them for a Jiggs' dinner on her way out. A hearty one-pot meal of salt beef, root vegetables and cabbage, it was an island favourite from the days when fish was everyday and beef rare and precious. These days, for additional red meat, many families participated in the moose cull that every year allotted up to fifty thousand licences towards the reduction in numbers of this feral ruminant. Generally, people shared their kill with neighbours or extended family. Half a moose was plenty to supplement the cod, salmon, trout, rabbit, and for some even bear and seal, that the natural seasons and cycles contributed to the larders of these isolated communities. But it was still salt beef, and salt beef only, that was the base of a pot of Jiggs' dinner.

Though she really liked to fish, Kayla was not by nature a hunter. But after talking with locals and coming to appreciate the long harsh months of winter and the limits of a one-hundred-day growth season, she had to acknowledge that this was an honest life. That harvesting your needs from the bounty of the woods and seas about you, and filling your cellars with potatoes, beets, carrots, turnips and cabbage, was the sort of simple provisioning she had often longed for. And she was impressed that the remote province of Newfoundland had regulated the hunting thoughtfully and in a steady progression of licensing throughout the year that always made something available, yet carefully limited the impact.

Kayla laid an envelope on the table. "Here are the keys to the truck, and a little something for its maintenance." As Audrey began to object Kayla laid her hand on the envelope. "I don't want to argue. The two of you have made this whole time so easy and … truly remarkable." She grinned. "And you were right. Can you imagine driving that track in the hire car? They'd have had a fit. And I would have been so anxious. So, thanks for the use of your car, and I hope it hasn't caused too much inconvenience."

Thomas looked at Audrey before he spoke. "To be honest, Kayla, it's been a right treat all round. You may not realise it but we'd had plenty of other offers for the cabin. Yours was the first we were willing to take. And your joy and appreciation, well it's been like feeling it ourselves all over again."

"Well then." Kayla put a second envelope on the table. "Perhaps you would like to take care of these. They're the keys to Stranger's Gate and I've been thinking you might like to enjoy it while I'm gone. I have no idea yet as to when I'll be able to return. Could be a year, could be three, and anyway I have no want or need to take it right out of your world. Unless you want me to, that is."

"I'll be thanking you now for both of us." Audrey said into the silence that followed, looking at Tom whose eyes had become very moist. "You can be sure we'll be keeping a good eye on it for you."

"I don't mean just that, you know. I want you to use the cabin, stay there anytime you can. Make the most of it, with all care but no responsibility. Any maintenance is all mine, and you mustn't hesitate to let me know what's needed. You've both taken such care of me, thought about things I wouldn't have known, even lent me your car. I'm deeply grateful."

Tom cleared his throat and picked up the envelope.

"You have warmed my heart, maid. We just wanted you to feel as safe as if you were in god's pocket, is all."

Man, these islanders had such a genuine old worldly and gentle manner that this time it was Kayla who had to clear her throat. Sometimes they seemed almost naïve, but it wasn't that either. They were just generous and kind folk, still linked to a way of life that was a faint memory in the current self-serving culture of modern times.

It had happened again, that unexpected intimacy of travel. Though most connections she had made were short-lived, suited only to that moment in time, these felt different. There was a real sense of longevity, a feeling that over the years to come, as she returned again to this island of her roots, they would grow and evolve into something strong and sustaining.

# Chapter 24

Kayla left the Trans-Canada Highway at Bishop's Falls, turning south onto Route 360 towards the Coast of Bays. What a relief to not have to worry about damaging the hire car now that she was back on tarred and well-graded roads.

Jan had made sure Kayla understood that the Bay d'Espoir Highway was 202 kilometres of lonely road linking central Newfoundland to the remote southern coast. Three hours or so from Gander to Harbour Breton didn't sound so far, not for an Australian anyway. Advice was to keep to the sixty- and eighty-kilometre speed limits to avoid damage from ice-scarred roads and wandering moose. Jan had also alerted her to the ghostly spectre of wild caribou ranging across the bog barrens. Kayla would pass by the Bay du Nord Wilderness Reserve, home to the largest remaining caribou herd in Northern America.

Thickets of birch, spruce and fir lined the highway. But it was the scattering of junipers that kept catching her eye. There was something softer in their foliage, something almost sentient as they leaned their higher tips towards the nearest ocean. She knew that longing. She could see them now, stretching above the conifers, seeking the solace of the sea.

The dense growth allowed an occasional flash of hidden water; a tease that gurgled and trilled like the river she felt sure ran periodically alongside the road behind the screen of needles.

Sixty kilometres in, the Northwest Gander River crossed the highway. Kayla slowed for the bridge just long enough to feel the pulse in her own veins of the arterial river below.

But Twillick Brook? The name itself was enough to tempt Kayla to pull over and take a break. Later she would learn that "twillick" was the local term for yellow-legged water birds, but a name like that was just too Jabberwockyish to pass on by.

She climbed down a gravelly slope and, shedding her sandals and jeans, stepped into the crystal-clear, tumbling water. Tiny rainbows hung in fine mist. Icy water tugged her thighs, the sharp current pulling at her feet as with curled toes she sought purchase in fine gravel. With cupped hands Kayla caught a taste of the bright stream, lifting it to her nose like a snifter of fine wine. These were waters of wetlands, earthy with memories of rich peat, moss and grains of old rock. Kayla splashed the morning's sweat from her face.

With ruddy legs and a tingle in her toes, Kayla returned to the car and dried off. Time was a constraint. Garnering supplies had taken longer than intended and much unknown still remained in the day. Hard to believe that at the end of this road she would meet her great-great-aunt. She had crossed half the world seeking the family thread that had bonded her to the mystery of her maternal grandmother. Tentative hope grew as the road slowly climbed. If ever there was a chance …

Finally the forests fell away, revealing a high plateau. Freed of the curtain of foliage, Kayla pulled off the road. As she got out of the car the wind whipped at her hair and clothes, the air rich with ozone and the metallic tang of impending rain. Almost tundra-like, there was no protection here for any living thing.

But what a view! Chains of ponds pockmarked a landscape of lichen, rock and stunted, weather-riven trees. Overhead, dense puffs of cumulus clouds fled strong high winds, shifting shadows across the land, the reflection on the ponds fluctuating from blue to black and back again.

Far to the south, hewn into the landscape, a tapering thread of silver reflected the water of the Bay d'Espoir fjord. From this distance Kayla could only wonder at the sheer power of massive creeping ice that had carved such a cleft through solid granite. After weeks in the lowlands of the north, she had arrived in a different country altogether.

The trail wound down to the sea through savaged outcrops. Kayla knew that around ten thousand years ago, the last of the glaciers slid off Newfoundland, creating these fissures and fjords with their sheer rock walls and steep slopes of pulverised rubble. Millions of tons of ground nutrient had been scraped into the sea, forming the rich marine feeding grounds of the Grand Banks. The European colonisation of Newfoundland was built on the profits from the prolific fish colonies that had flourished.

Once on the Connaigre Peninsula, a narrow causeway brought her into Harbour Breton. Like most coastal villages, it was spread around several coves tucked within a safe harbour. Resettlement from outports had created a suburban grid along the bottom of the bay, contrasting with the random aspect of the older sections scattered through the hills behind.

Shirl's Place, the B & B Audrey had recommended, was on the road to Gun Hill, an imposing mountain of grey scree overlooking Connaigre Bay. Shirl herself welcomed Kayla with a flourish, stepping back from the door to allow her entry. Multilevel shelves and shadow boxes laden with quirky collectables filled every available wall space. Trying not to knock anything with her pack, Kayla followed her host up steep, narrow stairs to her room. The sign on the door read *Mariner's Lookout*.

"Perhaps you'd like to freshen up and join us for supper in about an hour," Shirl offered.

"Thanks. That'd be great," Kayla assured her, even though it was only four in the afternoon. This island custom of early suppers still caught her stomach by surprise.

"Another hobbit house," Kayla muttered as she folded her body to sit on the short daybed built into a handcrafted bay window. The main bed was a double, as was common on the island, but Kayla would have to sleep on an angle to avoid hanging her feet over the edge. The room couldn't be more aptly named, though. There was a grand view right up the bay.

She'd timed it well. The weather was changing; the storm that had followed her into town was rapidly turning blue water into treacherous cold grey slate. The old house appeared solid as the wind howled its frustration, able to do little more than rattle windows and dance whitecaps across the bay. This would be a great place to hunker down for the night.

Dinner was fish and chips Newfoundland style: fresh, moist, lightly battered cod next to a mountain of browned chips skin intact, all drenched in gravy. Tonight's was strewn with stuffing, an island speciality of breadcrumbs and the herb, savoury. To the side sat a tiny tub of coleslaw, proportionate to the luxury that fresh vegetables must have been for centuries past. Sweet local blueberry pie followed. After a feed like that it wasn't too long till Kayla was ready to retreat.

The faint occasional sounds from downstairs of voices and quiet television intruded into her reverie. Watching the day fade from the sky, Kayla was surprised at the loss she felt at leaving the cabin. She sat a while before sleeping, simply grateful for the weeks she had been captivated, rapt in a profoundly nourishing weaving of solitude and intimacy.

# Chapter 25

The next morning Kayla had no appetite. Her adrenaline was up, the view over the now gentle sea unable to calm her nerves. It was still early, so after a cup of tea she drove out along the shoreline. Among the rocks she found a sheltered nook and sat till the caress of sun and salt-laden breeze steadied her breath. Kayla was well aware of the intensity she could inadvertently radiate. She had no desire to infect this meeting with Aunt Annie with any of the anxiety of the longing that had brought her so far from home.

Kayla had thought long and hard about sending a letter first, or even a phone call, but had decided to come in cold. If nothing else came of it, at the very least she would have the memory of the first response.

It was after ten when she finally knocked on the front door of the address on Newman's Point that Jan had provided. It took a long minute to open. A tiny hand appeared first. Small eyes peered out of a deeply lined face, forced to look upwards to seek Kayla's own. Kayla felt like a giant silhouetted against the bright sky.

"Can I help you?"

"I hope so. I'm looking for Annie Marie Harrison," Kayla offered with a tentative smile.

"Yes. That would be me."

"Mrs Harrison, my name is Kayla Lewis," she began, and then lost her momentum.

"Yes? Yes? What is it, maid?" Annie Harrison came further around the door.

"I don't mean to startle you, but I'm here from Australia. I'm Sandra's daughter. Sandra MacDonald."

"Yes?" Annie said, still uncertain, needing more.

"My Nan, that is my grandmother, well, she was your niece. Her maiden name was Mary Louise Porter."

Recognition swayed the old woman. Seeing Annie's eyes redden, Kayla reached out a steadying hand, but Annie gathered her own strength. With a sharp intake of breath Annie took a step forward and reached a thin arm up towards Kayla's cheek. Kayla bowed her head in unexpected reverence.

"Best let me see you then."

Slowly Annie lifted Kayla's chin till she could search her face. A slow smile that began in Annie's eyes gradually lifted into the creases of a face well practised in finding joy and pleasure in the world. Kayla warmed to her immediately, her relief almost physical. Already this was more than she had dared hope.

"Yes, my dear." Annie stepped back, making room. "Well, if you're Mary's girl then you best be coming in."

Kayla followed along a darkened hallway before stepping into a light-filled kitchen. Ah, the very heart of the home. She thought of Alice, and the women, and knew there was no better place for a conversation such as this.

"My goodness, it's a lot to consider. Perhaps a cup of tea would be just the thing," Annie suggested.

"That'd be lovely, thanks. Shall I call you Auntie? Or great-great-Aunt maybe?"

"Oh no, that's all way too old. Just call me Annie. Everyone else does."

Kayla tried not to stare as Annie put together a pot of leaf tea, clearly a well-practised ritual. Already they had something in common. Annie's clothes hung loose on her tiny frame. Short in stature, she had been stripped by age of any excess flesh she may have carried. Kayla looked around as they waited for the kettle to boil. The kitchen was simply furnished, a welcome relief after the clutter of collectables at the B & B. The table was as solid, its timber as old and dense as the house itself, legs turned and carved in the manner of days when the love of craft was valued more than the time given to the task. A few photos adorned one wall.

After placing their steaming cups on the table, Annie sat down to face her great-great-niece. They shared a smile shy with promise.

Kayla lifted her cup. "To finding family."

"To family lost, and their timely return," Annie responded, raising her own cup. "You knows I keep staring but I can hardly believe you're Mary's girl. I mean you're not, there was your mother came between. But you're hers all right, that I can see. You would have been, what, about ten when she passed?"

"I'd just turned nine."

Annie clicked her tongue. "Too soon for any good soul to leave this world. You must have missed her terribly."

Kayla struggled to speak. Even after all this time she had never found the words.

"Plenty of time for that later," Annie said, with the patience of the long-lived.

Grateful, Kayla nodded.

"Your grandmother, Mary, was my only niece, you see, the closest I would ever have to a daughter." Annie sighed. "I still sees herself and Daniel there on the wharf in Gaultois. September fifteen, 1951 it was. Never seen one so taken by a lad. Can you imagine, back in those times, travelling by ship all that way out to Australia?"

"Not really, though I do love any reason to be out on the ocean. Did you ever consider making the trip yourself? Just for a visit I mean," Kayla asked.

"Perhaps it could have been done, but … you know how the years pass, ever so quickly and unexpectedly – as do those we love. These days, well you can fly anywhere in a day. Back then it was the hardest thing, saying that kind of goodbye."

When Annie didn't go on, Kayla indicated the photos on the wall. "Are these your family?"

She saw Annie's troubled eyes, her intake of breath. Ah. No easy answer to that one then. She kind of wished she'd waited to be told. Too late now.

"That'll be our two boys. There on the left, is Edward, my Ted." Annie's thin wrist lifted towards the far photo. It was a finely framed image of a well-built young man dressed for the sort of cold Kayla had never known. The fur-lined hood of his bulky jacket framed a fresh face full of life, the flush of adventure in his cheeks. "Taken on his first trip out on the seal hunt, that was. All he'd ever wanted to do. He and Derek Rose joined the fleet in St John's. Eighteen thousand seals they brought back on their first trip. But our Ted never did return from the second."

"Oh, I'm so sorry. It must have been terrible for you."

Annie looked up at Kayla and nodded. "They say he went down between the ice. It was a dangerous thing, you see. Men lost every other voyage. He knew it, we knew it, but you had to let them go. We never did have his body to bury."

Kayla remembered the stories of how the men had to leap from floe to floe to cross the thawing, fractured ice. Of how sometimes as they landed the ice would break, or spin in the water, taking the unlucky sailor under the freezing sea. How quickly hyperthermia set in and how few were saved.

"And that one there be Colin, our youngest. And a fine fisherman he was too, just like his father. But when we lost the cod we lost many families from the island, including my own." Annie's voice was wistful. "Colin moved the family to British Columbia, where there was employment, and they could be near Lynn's parents. Those two are my grandchildren, Marcus and Hailey, and the little one our great-grandchild, Alexia."

"Do you still get to see them?"

"Oh, we exchange cards and an occasional phone call, but that is all for now. Perhaps one day the younger ones will be curious as yourself as to where they came from." They shared a smile, and in its warmth Kayla knew Annie was glad she had come to find her.

"I suppose it's a wall of memories when you speak of it like this," Annie continued thoughtfully. "But when you gets to my age you find you have outlived most of the folks you have known well. But I am grateful for the times I was born in. Goodness knows I have been gifted with much more than was ever lost."

They sat quietly for a moment while Annie topped up their tea.

"Perhaps, Kayla, you might tell us a little of yourself?"

Aware that her host might tire physically before either wearied of the conversation, Kayla briefly sketched in the chronological details. How she had moved to Ed's and learnt the ways of the farm and discovered a talent for dowsing. How she had travelled from there across a vast dry land almost unimaginable to one such as Annie, born of this island of mist and water. How Ed had ordained this journey; that his last wish for Kayla was for her to return to the land of her grandmother and connect with her roots. And now, here she was.

"And what a fine thing that is. But tell me, maid …" Annie stopped and held the moment till she caught Kayla's gaze steady with her own sparkling intent. "Would I be wrong in thinking there'd be more?"

Kayla shut her eyes wishing that when she opened them that Annie would be able read all the questions and memories that had inspired this quest.

As if reading her thoughts, Annie said, "Best give it a try, my girl. It's a long ways you've come, and I been waiting a long time to listen."

Kayla met Annie's gaze then, eyes wide, allowing the study. How she longed to be seen by this woman – but still she wondered if she dare. Then suddenly, merged and overlaid in the shared genes, she was there. Her Nan was right there, echoed in the lift of Annie's chin, in the fine bones of the cheeks and the turn of the brow. But mostly it was that glint or spark, or whatever it was, that was dancing in Annie's eyes, and the way they lifted at the corners as if just waiting for a reason to smile. Making Kayla smile, drawing her in, complicit with knowing there was another way to see the world; lit with the same wicked irreverence that things were never really as serious as others might have one think. The same eyes that had held her strong and safe, that had loved her and believed in her. Camouflaged in the folds of age that lined Annie's face, were the features Kayla had known better than the shape of her own hand.

"You are her! I mean, when I look at you I see … her. I … I remember …" Grief rose in Kayla. As if hurled through a fracture in time, she was back squatting by the fire in the mist that had come after the downpour, her Nan draining rain from the pan, and Kayla with dry twigs and steady breaths urging their fire back to life. Then leaning together, bathing in rain, sipping steaming hot tea … water dripping notes from the trees, onto their coats and their faces. And laughing, always laughing …

Words tumbling out, urgent, hungry to be told. "Every day she could get away, my Nan took me as far away into the bush as we could go. The wilder and scragglier the better. We'd wander along rivers and lakes and down to the ocean. Hidden places where we could be alone and away from everyone. No one else around to ask why we did the things we did. Nan taught me how to string a line to catch every kind of fish. We'd have a boil-up, as she used to call it. Sometimes we'd even leave our food at home on purpose and feed ourselves from fish and greens and weeds and wild blackberries that grew along the roadsides. Some days we'd light fires just for fun, just to sit around and talk." Kayla stopped, happy-sad.

"Special times indeed." Annie nodded.

"Oh Annie, she taught me so much … and I just loved her, you know. I still don't know how much she formed me … or if she loved me because I was different like her and we could be different together and never have to explain …" Kayla looked up at Annie. Wondering, gauging how much more she could say.

Annie was right there, quietly and intensely present. "Go on." she said.

"Yeah … but … and here's the thing." Kayla took a deep breath. "I was too young … she tried to share so much but I was too young to remember. Over the years things have come back to me, and now I understand that she knew it, had known it all along …"

"Knew what?" Annie gently prodded

"That for her and me everything was about water."

In the silence that followed, Annie reached for Kayla's hand and held it close in her own, offering unspoken safety and encouragement.

"That is … through water is how we both feel the world, as if the water is our blood, the rivers and creeks our veins, and the oceans our home. I can really only speak for myself, but I know that's exactly how she felt too. That's why she took me to all those places. That it was some kind of training, as if she knew she wasn't going to be here long and she had to squeeze every last drop of her knowledge into my little being. She showed me how to feel the thousand ways of water. How it energises and oxygenates, gurgling through rapids and rocks. How it freezes and melts and even disappears into steam, yet always comes back to its simple self. And how it remembers …" Kayla stopped, surprised at the torrent, but not so surprised at the intensity.

"Don't get me wrong, Annie. I love my mum and dad. I do, but sometimes … it's as if all the special parts of my Nan skipped a generation. Since she's been gone it's been hard to see my reflection in the rest of the world. Without her … I haven't really known where I belong."

"You have always been one of us, child. Let this be the welcome home you dreamed of."

For a long moment all Kayla could do was wait for the rush of emotion to subside. "I guess that's why I am here. That the only way I would ever find *it*, or even be able to define what *it* was really all about would be by going backwards. Back to where my Nan came from all those years ago. Back into the stories she tried so hard to share with a little girl too young to listen. Times when people's welfare was as bound up in their relationship to the earth and oceans as mine seems to be." Kayla stopped, drew breath.

"There's no denying it," said Annie. "Our Mary had a gift, and it seems she has made it yours. Perhaps the reason she had to leave was that she had to bring you into the world. Life has a funny way of getting just what it needs."

Quietly contemplating that thought, Kayla made another pot of tea.

After they were settled Annie faced her squarely. "Now I believe it's time you tell me about your dreams."

"What do you mean? Which ones?"

Annie chuckled. "I think you be knowing exactly which ones, my girl."

Kayla closed her eyes. When she opened them again Annie was still waiting, her brown eyes sharp with anticipation.

"How did you know?"

Again Annie laughed. "How could I not? It's what's really brought you home, isn't it?"

"Yes … I guess." Kayla conceded. Where to begin? "For as long as I can remember, I've dreamt of water. But not normal dreams. On those nights it's like I'm fully awake and I remember it all and they seem as real as this table … or this room … or you. And they're always in or near water, in oceans or rivers or waterholes. Mostly they begin all murky, sort of obscured or motley like rainy windows. And there are almost always fish. Salmon and others I now know to be cod. Huge, old beings that seem calm … and kind … and sort of knowing." Kayla stopped, and laughed, suddenly a little shy.

Annie settled further back in her chair. "Go on," she encouraged.

"Most of the dreams are silent, or should I say without human speech," Kayla continued. "Slow, careful journeys diving down into the strange worlds of very deep ocean. Other nights it's just fun, swimming and surfing with all sorts of creatures. These ones shift between bright sun and muted light and they're energetic and exhausting all at once. Those days I've had to drag myself around, all worn out from the night before."

Annie nodded, willing her on. "And?"

"And then there's … Nunik."

Annie clasped her hands together and rocked where she sat barely able to contain her excitement. "You knows it. You just knows it."

"Who is she?" Kayla whispered.

"Who is *she*?" Annie chuckled, rosy with delight. "Why, child, *she* would be the spirit that has come down to you through all the generations of women who came before. Even from a child your great-great-grandmother was such a creature of water everyone naturally called her Nunik. It's the Inuit word for a female seal, you see, and that's how she was, slipping in and out of water that would kill the rest of us with cold. And just as playful as a seal I might add, always finding ways to bring people together even in the darkest of nights. I'd be right now, wouldn't I, that this would be the one who comes to you?"

Kayla nodded. Annie knew. Without any explanation Annie understood her deepest, darkest secret life. Could Nunik really be the very same spirit that had guided the life of her grandmother, her grandmother's grandmother, and the grandmother before that? And before her, all the way back down her line? Kayla loved the progression: great-grandmother, grandmother, granddaughter. For a brief, deeply grounding moment, Kayla felt a place that was hers and hers alone, snug between those who had been before and those yet to come.

"It's why I'm here. Why finding you, it's …" When Kayla looked up, the expression on Annie's face was pure cheek.

"Already far more than you bargained for, I'm betting." Annie was still laughing to herself as she came carefully to her feet. "But for now I'm all worn out with excitement."

Kayla stood up, trying not to react to the abrupt dismissal when she saw the droop of weariness in the bent back.

Annie grasped Kayla's arm and, with head aslant, looked up at her with an expression she would come to treasure. From under a questioning brow Annie's eyes were glistening with an invitation to mischief, adventure and all ends of possibility. "Do you happen to be driving yourself then? Yes? Then perhaps we could pop out a bit later, just you and I?"

Not even sure what she was grinning about or what she was about to agree to, Kayla found she was suddenly buzzing with heightened anticipation. "That'd be wonderful. I would love that."

"Why don't you go and have a bit of a look about or a rest or whatever it is you need to do, then come on by and pick me up about four this evening?"

"OK. See you then." Kayla leant in and kissed the soft skin of Annie's cheek. "I'll just let myself out."

"Make sure to be back now." Annie called after her.

Kayla laughed – as if she'd ever let this chance go by. "Don't worry. I will," she said, pulling the door closed behind her.

# Chapter 26

After the muted light of the cottage, the day was all glare. Slipping behind sunglasses, Kayla grabbed lunch in town and headed out to the end of a small promontory. Overlooking the rolling waves was a grassy knoll, lush and green with a sprinkling of tiny wildflowers. She lay back into its soft cushioning, drifting with the clouds and the wind and the awoken memories of her Nan, the woman who had had such a profound effect on all she had become.

Dead on four o'clock, Kayla was back at the door.

"Prompt little thing you are," Annie muttered as she let Kayla in.

She was indeed. Kayla had always reckoned that being late undervalued the time of both parties. But she wasn't the only one ready to go. Under Annie's guidance Kayla gathered coat, umbrella and walking cane "just in case" and they were on their way by five past the hour.

"You'll be wondering where we are off to then?" Annie asked with that mischief in her smile.

"Well, yes, I am. But as of now, I'd go anywhere with you."

Annie laughed. "Ah that's the spirit."

Although barely able to see over the dashboard, Annie directed Kayla to turn onto a narrow sidetrack that ran alongside Deadman's

Bay. "Oh my goodness, she is looking glorious today. That's it, take this track here," Annie exclaimed, clapping her hands with excitement as Kayla, for a brief precious moment, glimpsed the ecstatic wonder of the child Annie had once been, still powerfully present in this woman, in this elder she had just begun to know.

Kayla drove slowly till Annie directed her into a side turn that took them almost to precipice's edge.

"Pull in here, maid. I'm thinking this'll be a fine place to sit a while."

Steep cliffs fell away to hidden coves. Defiant stone islands adorned the rich blue summertime seas that Newfoundlanders are so blessed with. Gentle warmth radiated from the late afternoon sun. Light winds delicately laced with summer and salt drifted through their open windows.

For a time they sat, sharing a peace that revealed the faint brush of waves on the beach below and an occasional whisper of the grass.

"Some have asked me where I wish to be when death is near. Today I would say to them, I am here," Annie began, without turning. "I have thought to myself, that on a day such as this, I could simply slip into the ocean's embrace, washing up here and there at the whim of the tide and moon." She smiled, almost at herself. "Perhaps I am simply tiring of this body."

"I'm sure she'd be honoured to hold you, and keep you as her treasure." Kayla said softly.

"You are, are you lass? Well, you may just be one of us after all." Annie turned to Kayla. "I have wondered what it is that you know of your Newfoundland family?"

"Only bits and pieces from Nan. I learned more from my friend, Jan, from Carmenville. She's the one who found out where you were. Mum said that what she knew was unlikely to be true, and that we were the last of the line and that all Nan's family would probably be dead by now." Kayla leant back in her seat. "I've since wondered why she said those things."

"Dead and buried, eh? I say not yet." Annie laughed. "But I am thinking that your mother only wished to protect you from things she couldn't understand, and quite possibly feared."

"Yeah, I sort of knew that." Kayla acknowledged. "And I suppose I was a somewhat strange kid." She laughed. "But back to my Nan, I do remember parts of stories, and when I think about them I get images that I would have made up as I listened to her talk. When Nan wasn't silent she talked a lot – and I mean a lot." They laughed, together. And that was nice. "No really, she did. And though I don't remember any order or sequence to her telling, everything was always connected one way or another; the sea, the woods and the animals and … well…you know …" She looked at Annie.

"Know what?" Annie asked, and she had that look again.

"You know … magic and stuff."

"Oh, that," Annie said, rocking with delight. "I expected no less from our girl and there'll be time for that later. But tell me, what you do know of your heritage, particularly that long line of women who wished you into being?"

How could four words hold such power? *Wished you into being.* Never had Kayla felt so wanted … or connected … or justified. Then, as if they reached out from ages past, she felt swaddled in arms, enveloped in a cloud-soft blanket woven of exquisite tenderness …

Kayla swallowed hard before she could speak. "I know nothing really," she was finally able to confess. "Even on Dad's side. I know some about the men but none of the women."

"Is that so?" Annie scoffed. "Well, let me tell you, maid. There'll be no leaving the women out of the Newfoundland story. Oh no my dear, not in my telling there won't."

Kayla couldn't help loving this feistiness. This, at last, really was her blood. "Great. Then let's start at the beginning, please."

"Not quite sure where that was, but … I imagine you've heard tell the story of my grandmother, Elen, and how she came to the island?" Annie asked. Kayla shook her head. "No? Well, it's past time you did."

Annie took a deep breath and settled back into the seat, preparing for the telling of a long-ago tale. Kayla grinned. This was one of the stories she had ached for.

"It had been a terrible few days for many in Hermitage Bay and all along the Bay d'Espoir," Annie began. "A powerful storm had swept into the fjord, unexpected you see, battering the coast and any caught out of safe harbour. One night a Spanish ship came to grief on the standing rocks near the passage into Pushthrough Harbour. When the boats could finally put out, it was a mere slip of a girl they found clinging to the rocks, near drowned and all fevered from the chilling. No other had survived that dreadful night. And so it was that your great-great-great-grandmother was brought home to Long Island."

Annie shivered, distant with remembering.

"She spoke neither English nor French. Just a touch of Spanish, mixed with a language no one knew. Best they could make out was that her name was Elen. It was the good heart of Mari Madec who took her in. Before too long it was discovered she was already with child, though barely more than a girl herself. And so it was, that in March 1882, Elen wed Ewan, Mari and Jak's son, a good lad willing to take both mother and child. Born within the week – some have said it was that child's need to be birthed that brought Elen safely to land that day.

"They named the child Mairin, meaning star of the sea. And

what a strange little star she was. From the moment Mairin could crawl, she could swim, and let me tell you that is not a common thing for a Newfoundlander. And wild! Barely four years of age, she slipped her mother's grasp and, without any warning, leapt into turbulent water and disappeared. Well, everyone thought Mairin was forever lost, but after more minutes than is natural, that child came to the surface waving and laughing without the least bit of fear. It was then she was given the pet name, Nunik. And never was one more fitting." Annie halted in her commentary, taking a long moment for a long ago past.

Kayla's heartbeat raced as she hung on every word. "Go on," she whispered.

"But Elen never did truly recover. It was a sad day when she died of a weak lung with the child just nine years old."

"Same as me when I lost my Nan."

"That be so," Annie acknowledged. "But as for little Mairin? Despite being of such tender age, it was said that young girl forged her own unique way through the sheer strength of her nature, as if her spirit was born of the water itself. She grew into a fierce protector of the creatures of the sea.

"Mairin had a goodness few could resist, growing into a fine talent for delivering babies and brewing potions, and curing many whose hope was all but lost. At the end of frozen winters, it would be she who would be the first to find the green shoots of spring and quell the curse of scurvy. Isolated as we were, every village needed such a woman in those times. Even those who had feared her for the blood of a witch, were grateful when her healing touched their families."

Nodding to herself, Annie fell into a reverie, as if adrift in memories of times past. Willing her to continue, Kayla waited out the silence as she gazed over the sparkling sea, transported in time, awed not only by the depths of the bottomless well she had slipped into, but how exciting the fall.

In her own good time, Annie opened her eyes. "It has been an age since I have spoken of such things. Now tell me, young Kayla, where were we?"

"You were telling me about your mother, Mairin."

"Ah yes. Now there was a woman of her own mind. Despite her father's urgings, our mother never would consent to be married, would never have allowed herself to be so answerable to another. An itinerant trapper, name of Duncan McCall, fathered both my sister and me. We came to understand my mother never wanted him for more than the gift of her children. Mairin was twenty-one when I was born and twenty-four when she had my sister, Stella. Then our father was gone forever."

"Did you ever look for him, your dad, I mean?" Kayla wondered aloud.

"There was a time later in life, that Stella searched the few registers she could find, but there was little ever recorded. We did hear he'd been known for his furs around Deer Lake, but it seems he'd been a woodsman with little use for the outside world and left barely a trace of his existence.

"So it was my sister and I spent our young years at Mairin's side, much in the manner of you and your Nan. And try she did, but we weren't very old before both Stella and I knew that there was something our mother sought that neither of us could give … or had … or wanted as much as she. Oh, believe me, my sister and I have the blood in our own ways. But it comes with a price, this otherworldliness. It set our mother apart, and I know she felt terribly alone throughout her life." Annie reached up and stroked Kayla's cheek. "Already I see this brush of solitude in you. Despite this … other connection, there is also … an aloneness. So it was that Stella and I made other choices, more conventional choices perhaps, forgoing a life of honouring 'The Remembering' as our mother would say, as we settled for husbands and a more traditional family."

Annie stopped and wiped moisture from her eye. Kayla would never know if it was the unresolved regret of her story or the touch of the cool wind that blew through her open window.

But after a minute she began again. "It was when Mary was born to Stella that everything changed. Just as soon as that child could walk on her chubby little legs, she was the shadow of her grandmother. Cold, hot, wet or dry, Mary would do whatever it took to be at Mairin's side traipsing through ice and snow and deep into the woods. That child heeded all the oral history and lore of our people given by her grandmother, and she would spin it back in a way Stella and I had never been able.

"Our Mary grew wild and strong, and we were all sure that one day she would take up the mantle; that in time she would become the keeper of the knowledge, and the magic the rest of us would only ever glimpse.

"But then it was that Daniel MacDonald arrived, a strapping young lad all the way from Australia – came by chance to our little island. In no time young Mary was leaving to cross the world with him. Even so, nobody imagined it would be forever."

"But it was." Kayla whispered.

"Yes, my dear, that it were. But look at you, sitting right here with me now. Who would ever have thought? Mary's very own granddaughter. All those years passed and you have come back home. Drawn by what, I do wonder."

Annie's searching gaze was unsettling. Under the probing scrutiny all Kayla could do was shake her head. It was so hard to find the words.

"It's because this is where Nan became all that she was. Everything that was special about her had come from some other place far, far away from where I knew her. And her past had to hold the keys to understanding the truth of me … of us … she and I. Why we see things … and feel things the way we do."

"So it's the truth you be seeking then is it, lass? Can't fault that. If my mother taught me anything, it is that truth comes in infinite colours and stories and moments." Annie reached for Kayla's hand. "Perhaps that's enough for today. Let's do this again tomorrow, shall we?"

Oh yes. Kayla nodded. "Tomorrow sounds great."

For Kayla, generations of her women had come alive, embodied by Annie's story and love. With nowhere else to be, they sat a while longer pondering the resonance of such memories, cradled in the soundscape of the shoreline and the sweet scents drifting on the summer breeze.

# Chapter 27

Over the next few days Kayla visited Annie whenever she could. Between times she explored the harbour, swam in coves, rivers and ponds, and walked the stony shorelines. There was so much she longed to know and so little time.

"So who was Elen really?" Kayla asked one morning, as they both sat back with cuppas in hand, shafts of morning sun reflecting sparkling seas.

"Ah, the question for which I can give little answer and wish more than anything that I could." Annie shook her head. "Strangely, I barely knew my father either, yet I have grieved not knowing my grandmother more. Perhaps this is where that elemental bond, what you call the magic, came from. For it's likely her people were from those far northern realms of ice and snow where the whole world is water, wind and weather, in one way or another."

"Makes sense," Kayla agreed. "But the other villagers must have been open to it too. I know that there was a lot of superstition back then. Do you know why the Madecs and the other families of Piccarie chose to make their lives in such a remote harbour, on such a remote island in the first place?"

"Now this I can tell you." Annie nodded. "Along with their

Christian faith, these families were known to have held to the old Celtic ways of honouring the natural world. It was after persecution in the mid seventeen hundreds that the Madecs sailed away from Brittany, seeking the freedom to follow their own beliefs. They first settled on the Avalon Peninsula, but when the French surrendered Placentia to the British, the small community moved to Piccarie on Long Island."

"So they were rebels of a kind?"

"Yes, my dear. Some would say that and many more would agree." Annie chuckled. "Some might say that much of Newfoundland was pioneered by those willing to buck authority. Fishermen and sailors alike chose the hardship of life here rather than return to the terrible poverty back across the Atlantic. To this day, Newfoundlanders place little faith in government to service the good of the people themselves. But that's another story for another day. You can see how, with such a background, it was not difficult for the village to accept, even come to respect, the strange, mystical nature of my mother."

Annie reached out and squeezed Kayla's hand before continuing. "I'm sorry to say that most records and registries from Piccarie are long gone, lost in fires and other calamities. But what we do know is that over the centuries there have been all kinds of intermarriages. Here on the south coast, we were renowned for the pirates and buccaneers who took refuge among the fjords and islands. Then there were the travellers such as my father who came for the fishing and furs, as well as the Beothuk and Mi'kmaq people whose ancestors had roamed these islands long before Europe knew of their existence.

"But change was coming, Kayla. There was no turning back the tide of progress. We had been a self-sufficient people with a way of life all our own. Outport life was hard, there's no denying, and the winters long and severe, but when fish prices became too low to pay our way, and the catches ever smaller … well, it was a dreadful thing."

"I've read of the terrible poverty," said Kayla, "and how tuberculosis took hold right across the island."

"Those of us that who lived those times will never forget. Many we loved were lost. A terrible disease in a time of terrible hunger." Annie shook her head. "But now, my girl, it's having me remember there are some photo albums I haven't looked at in years. Perhaps you might see what you can find in the spare room wardrobe."

Stories flowed from the older woman, inspired by the remnant collection of aged, grainy, mostly black-and-white photos. Kayla pored over each and every one, searching for her Nan, the face she most longed to see. She was nowhere to be found.

The next morning, unable to sleep, Kayla rose before the dawn. She slipped from her room, down softly moaning stairs and out into the day. The morning was perfectly still. She strode through quiet streets invigorated – no, more than that, intoxicated as she drew deeply on fresh, dew-moistened air ripe with Atlantic brine. As if forgotten, yet so, so familiar, every breath was triggering receptors to nourishment as ancient as her line itself.

At Kayla's suggestion they had planned a picnic for today. Nothing fancy, just a sandwich and thermos shared on a bench at the ocean's side. After that first trip out together, Kayla had realised how Annie ached for the opportunity to be close to the water, sharing a lingering lunch with nothing more than a warm rug over her knees, the music of the waves, and wheeling gulls in her ears.

But Annie also had a plan. After they packed away their wrappers and empty cups, she directed Kayla back around a few turns and out along a narrow gravel track. Scrawny, savaged tuckamores clung to cliff tops, their twisted limbs like creatures frozen in a sorcerer's nightmare.

"Just keep going?" Kayla asked as the road surface deteriorated further.

Annie nodded. "Yes, my dear." They didn't speak much after that. Although Annie constantly scanned the country they were travelling through, her focus lay somewhere further ahead. She was a woman with a mission, and Kayla was happy just to be at the wheel.

Nearly twenty minutes on, Annie directed Kayla to turn down an even narrower, stonier track. Despite Annie's restless enthusiasm, Kayla crawled the hire car slowly over the rough surface. Soon they had left the open ground for a path between two large boulders that lined their way like guardians of honour. Just as Kayla was seriously wondering about turning back, they were there.

"Stop. Stop right here," Annie commanded.

"No worries," Kayla readily agreed. Annie drew on her coat and, leaning heavily on her cane, crossed the uneven terrain to the cliff's edge. Kayla held back from reaching out to hold onto her. If Annie couldn't choose the nature of her own risks in her nineties, then when would she ever?

It was spectacular. From high above the water, they gazed over a panorama of islands and coves, craggy cliff-sides and stony beaches, all interwoven with a deep blue sea. Atlantic gulls, terns and broad-winged seabirds glided and called in the wind. It was a sound so different from those of home. Kayla was taken to scenes of old British films depicting the islands of Orkney, or Skye, where only the hardy survived and only the lonely gulls bore witness.

After several minutes Annie leaned on Kayla's arm, drawing her towards a flat rock tucked snug in a hollow in the lee of the wind.

"Come. Let's sit for a bit."

Annie took Kayla's hand and drew it into her lap, cradling it in both her own. They sat like this for a while as the ocean below swelled and broke to a pulse echoed on far-distant shores, moving to a rhythm as changeable yet as constant as the tides.

"Thanks be to you, Kayla," Annie began, squeezing her hand. "You have brought a completion to my time I never imagined possible. This morning I woke with a sense of this frail old body as a bridge that spanned many generations. I never had thought of myself as the strong one but then I saw that, for our family, I alone remain as the one constant through eras of unrelenting change, the link between one kind of existence and another."

Kayla went to speak but Annie tugged her hand sharply. She then understood that it was Annie who had made this particular moment, was holding this space, and asked nothing of Kayla but to be truly heard.

"I was born into a time when our earth provided in all but the harshest of seasons and lands," Annie began. "Any willing to work with their own hands experienced nourishment of both body and spirit by the simple act of sharing with the earth and each other. Everybody's welfare was determined by our willingness to participate in our community. Our thoughts and caring extended to all of our village and beyond, and in return we knew that we were held by others. Times that, when push came to shove, all children were our children, all women our sisters, all men our brothers, and the earth our mother. When little was enough, and we were grateful for each day, each meal, and each life taken to sustain our own."

The sound of the waves below filled the space between words

as Kayla drew in the deep nourishment of rising ozone. What a life it must have been, even with all the hardship. How she longed for those simple times, for the bonds that would have been forged from necessity … and the adversity itself.

"Don't get me wrong now," Annie continued. "When you put any bunch of folks together there will always be politics and dissent and envy. We are strange creatures, we humans. Perhaps we have always been a mixture of those who believe they know, those who seek, and those who ask little, hope for more, and often accept far less. Yet, despite those differences, when each and every person's welfare depends on the welfare of all, well that is a circumstance that has been known to bring out the best of us. And let me tell you, you cannot put a value on that in a life."

Annie stopped, and looked far out to sea, as if filling herself with wisps of distant memory. Resisting the urge to comment, Kayla held to her silence. There was nothing to do but wait.

"Growing up with my mother was a strange and wondrous beginning. Our home was hung with pungent herbs and charms, busy with a steady stream of those whose need was healing, or a little help to sway life to follow their wants.

"What you call magic was just part of our ordinary days. Our mother called it 'the oneness'. She would have added something along the lines that there can be no one, without the other. Every entity, be it a person, creature, ocean, tree, mountain or brook is born as an expression of nature herself in all her fullness, each intrinsically interwoven in the great tapestry only by the grace of our place in the whole. Like a wave or a leaf, an icicle or a snowdrop, we are birthed into being for our given time, we die, we return to the whole, and we would do well to not think of ourselves as more than that." Annie stopped.

"I really like that," Kayla said into the lull.

Annie chuckled. "I thought you might. I'll be thinking it's pretty much how you see the world too, isn't it."

Kayla nodded. "Nothing else makes sense to me. I can't imagine how the complex web of life could exist any other way." Her great-great-grandmother was coming alive in Annie's words. Not only of kin, but of like mind. This thinking, this way of being and seeing the world, was in her very own cells themselves. She turned away before Annie saw the quiver of emotion in her lips, but it was too late.

"Come now. Look at me," Annie insisted.

Reluctantly, Kayla turned.

"Ah my girl, it's blood you are and there'll be no doubting that now. But let me share more, for the future my mother feared more than any other was that humankind would come to believe in its own superiority above all else. She would say, 'He is the most foolish of men who wishes to will the world into submission based on the judgement of a mind that fears its own limitations.' And so it has come to pass. The earth is being ravaged to the edge of her endurance. My mother foresaw this and mourned for what was to come. She could see no way to slow it and that was a sadness she took to an early grave."

Annie rested her head on Kayla's shoulder and squeezed her hand as they sat a while. Despite the physical presence of her great-great-aunt, Kayla ached, so deep in her body it felt like it was in her soul itself, for a relationship with the living, breathing mentor of Mairin she could never have.

After a time, Annie cleared her throat and, as if pulling herself together, sat up straight and strong. "It is forty-one years since Mairin, or Nunik as you have come to know the spirit of her, returned to the great ocean of the ancestors. Today I wish to share with you, dear Kayla, what I remember of The Remembering." Her smile was slightly aslant with melancholy, but her eyes flashed with that glimmer of imminent excitement that sent a shivering thrill through Kayla's spine.

"Come. Take my arm if you will. I may not have been the one she hoped for, but I am certainly my mother's daughter."

Slowly they made their way again to cliff's edge. The wind had increased a little, giving them a slight sway where they stood.

"Now, let us take a moment to prepare, to allow your spirit to travel further than your mind possibly can," Annie said as she gripped Kayla's hand with a strength that belied the ageing physical body. Then, there it was again, that powerful link of kin; the same feeling as when the grown hand of her Nan had clutched Kayla's tiny child's hand all those years before. Inspiring trust and willingness and the courage to enter further and further into the adventure. Even as she calmed her racing heart, Kayla had never been more ready for this day.

"Close your eyes and take a few gentle breaths," Annie said softly. "That's the way. Slow it down. Now feel the wind's caress across your cheek. How it lifts and drifts though your hair, the way it's playing with the loose edges of your clothing. Let your ears capture the murmur of the ocean and the slow grind of the rocks. Slowly, slowly, in and out until it becomes you and you become it. Taste the sharp tang of the salt entering your nostrils, feel them flare at its touch. Draw it down, down, down deeply into your lungs till there is no separation."

Minutes passed. Kayla breathed till she found a rhythm with the waves, her breath swelling and falling, swelling and falling until she was caught in a stream of forever. Till she could taste the brine as it mingled with the moisture of her mouth and the salts of her skin, until she could feel how the wind turned to play over the surfaces of her body. Till she knew with her feet the way the cliff fell away to the water and how the ocean caressed the shore, teasing the tumbled rocks below. Till her ears sang with the whisperings of the land she inhabited, and the gulls' calls hung in distant skies.

Annie took one last deep slow breath and turned to Kayla.

"Now, slowly open your eyes."

They stood that moment together, sharing something neither could see but both knew had come.

"I am the daughter of the wind, Kayla. As you are water, I am air." With that Annie turned her face into the breeze. It swirled around her body, which seemed to lift and swell in its ethereal embrace.

"Join with me as you will. Take whatever part comes to you. There is no wrong way."

Ever so softly, Annie began to sing. Almost a chant, it soon merged with the rhythm of her breathing, gradually becoming louder as if the song itself was giving strength to the singer. The wind's intensity increased, making Kayla glad of the grip she held on Annie's arm. And still Annie sang.

Gradually, Kayla's mind surrendered to the trance. Without will she began to sing, weaving her voice with Annie's. Again the wind lifted from the water, then turned to come from behind to carry their song far out over the silvery surface.

Patterns appeared as the wind tripped and danced across the bright ocean, trilling and thrilling the surface, shifting a palette of blue and black and silver across a canvas as vast as the distant horizon yet as intimate as the breeze returning piquant with the kiss of salt and seaweed.

Together their entwined voices rose, growing in intensity, as did the play of the wind ruffling and teasing at the water, shaping in it the closest to a transcript, a musical score, of a symphony of air that Kayla could ever imagine. After some time, dark shapes appeared, shadow play from the depths drawn briefly into the mesmerising dance. Then all at once, several spouting spumes burst into the air, as one after the other a pod of whales broke the surface, a tail here, a long slow sliding back there.

As Annie's voice faded, so too did Kayla's. Gradually the surface calmed and the shadows sank back into the deep. Still they stood on cliff's edge, Kayla clutching Annie's arm with a fierce determination to never let this woman go. This was her blood alright.

Finally, without words, they turned to each other. Annie was exhausted. Kayla folded the finely aged body of her great-greataunt into the strong arms of her youth and hugged her close.

Carefully Kayla helped Annie back towards the car. As they settled into the seats Annie turned to Kayla, her eyes filled with joy and just a little pride that needed no explanation. Rightly so, Kayla thought as she drove them both home. With only a passing reluctance, Annie let Kayla lift her depleted body into bed and tuck her in. All through the night Kayla sat beside her, unable to settle, brimming with love for this extraordinary and generous woman.

# Chapter 28

Kayla woke, startled by a harsh cough from the bed. She lifted her cheek from where it had pressed into the wooden frame and unfurled her stiff body. Somewhere in the long hours before dawn she had slept, dreamless and still. In the muted light Annie's body looked even smaller, little more than a rumple in a toss of blankets. Kayla crept to the window. Traces of dawn coloured the horizon. Nights were for wandering the stars, Annie had said, and though she had curtains, she only closed them at night in the coldest of winter, or in the middle of the day when she needed to rest.

"There'll be no need to creep about. I'm not dead yet."

Kayla turned back to the bed. "Well, good morning to you too, Auntie."

She perched on the edge and stroked fine white hair gently back from the paper-thin skin of Annie's forehead. Annie's eyes fluttered open then closed again.

"So tired today," she muttered.

"Of course you are," Kayla whispered. "There's nothing needs doing right now. Just rest, sleep a little more."

Annie stirred. "But you must—"

"Shh now, it's all good. I'm not going anywhere. I'll be right here when you wake." That seemed to reassure her and under Kayla's tender caress, Annie slipped back into sleep.

Kayla stood, acutely aware of her height, towering over the little old body that lay so still in the bed. Three generations had added near half a metre of height to her genetic line. What a miracle to have found this woman still articulate and empowered from the learning given nearly a century before. Annie had witnessed so much change, lost so much as the years had marched relentlessly on. It had been a long life steeped with a courageous capacity for give and take.

It was nearly ten o'clock when Annie stirred again. With only minor protest she allowed Kayla to fuss about, settling her into her favourite comfy chair in front of the living room window. It wasn't so cold, but in her exhausted state Annie's fingers were icy. Kayla found a bit of kindling and a couple of logs and soon had the wood stove burning.

She handed Annie a hot cuppa and pulled up a chair next to her aunt's. "A warm fire, love of family, a grand view of sea and sky, and a fresh cup of tea. Doesn't get much better by my reckoning."

Annie's agreement came as a smile. Though her face was still pale, the light in her eyes reflected a spirit still uplifted, still connected to realms beyond words or physical touch.

Conversation came slowly. An easy silence stretched between them, nothing more important that they needed to be doing, nowhere else they ought to be.

"I hadn't known why I was waiting," Annie said eventually, continuing to stare out. "Why it was that I had lived so long beyond those I loved most in this life."

Kayla covered Annie's hand with her own.

"I last sang the wind after my mother died, thinking I never would again. For a long while I was lost in the mourning. Not just for herself, but there was the grief for our Mary being gone so far away, and for the heritage that our mother and all those women of knowing had longed to pass forward. Who would remember and teach the connection between the worlds of spirit and humankind? The world about was changing so fast and the young ones, our young ones, had little want to know. It was only ever Mary that held the hope."

Annie nodded to herself, then turned, lifted Kayla's hands to her lips and kissed them. "Now here you are, my love, as tall and strong as any I've seen."

Kayla laughed. It wasn't the first time she'd been told that.

"You might not have my height, Annie, but what you did was incredible. Yesterday …" Kayla stopped, searching for words. "They were there, Auntie, all those women were right there with us. Our line. And I was with them, even as I was standing at your side right there on the cliff. Only with them I was just a wee thing wrapped in a bundle of cloth, being held and treasured by each as I was passed through time itself. I could feel caresses of loving hands all over my body, my ears filled with whispers and wishes of encouragement and hope … and love. For the first time since Nan died, I felt such a fierce and unshakable bonding … making me yours … just like I was Nan's."

Annie's chin quivered as her thin little hands gripped Kayla's own with all that words could not convey.

"Finally, it's all beginning to make sense – what I've felt inside me, what I've dreamed of, what I've found myself able to do without ever knowing the source. I'm so grateful that you waited, Aunt Annie. I'm just sorry it took me so long."

"Ach, sorry be damned. These things only happen in their own good time. Would you have been ready to sing with me before now? I doubt it. However, my weariness is bone deep, and I live in no uncertainty that my time is near over."

Kayla went to argue but Annie brushed her objections away with the flick of her hand.

"Do not waste time arguing. I have no time to teach what is mine to give, but these days spent together have shown me you already have all you need, and more besides. What you may not have been born with, our Mary has already instilled. However, if you are ready, I have one last thing I'd like to give you."

Kayla choked back an overwhelming sense of impending loss and nodded.

"Go to the chest of drawers in the second bedroom. In the third drawer you will find a wooden box. Please bring it to me if you will."

Kayla did as she was asked, taking an extra moment in the privacy of the bedroom to gather her courage. So much was happening.

Annie took the box and laid it in her lap. The box was old, the hand-carved engravings scarred with use and time. Opening the lid revealed a bag of soft hide.

Lifting it carefully, Annie held it to her heart before passing it to Kayla. "Feel that," she encouraged. "I can't imagine you've ever held seal hide before. This is the most waterproof pelt nature creates. Nothing keeps you as warm and dry. I am absolutely certain that the treasure it contains was always meant for you."

"For me?" Kayla hesitated.

"My mother gave it to me just before she died. I would know, she said. And now I do. I place it in your keep, Kayla. Treasure it as your birthright. I pass it to you with it all the blessing of the winds, the water and the deep well of wonder that still inspires this frail old body."

Kayla opened the leather thong that secured the bag. Carefully she drew out an intricately carved section of horn or antler.

"What you have there is a remnant of the tusk of a great sea lion, hollowed and carved," Annie began. "These are the creatures that ensured the survival of my grandmother's people, from the days when their entire world consisted of endless cycles of ice and snow."

As Kayla turned the tusk up, another parcel slid from within. Kayla grabbed for it as it fell, wrapping her hand tightly around the shape. Instantly she was taken back to the full-bodied breasted seal and the gift of her dreaming.

"Nunik!" Kayla had spoken aloud without realising.

Annie laughed aloud for the first time that day. "Yes, maid. Seems she has always been right with you."

Although there was a fine layer wrapped around the item there was no question in Kayla's mind. This was the same shape Nunik had handed her in the dream. Inside was the spiral core from the inside of a deep-sea shell, carved even more intricately than the tusk, not with animals but with three symbols. It fitted perfectly in Kayla's hand.

Annie nodded her approval. "This is an object of power, Kayla. Mind it carefully. Be aware it comes with a calling to something larger than yourself and your own worldly needs. But you already know this. The only question is how you will use this gift, and perhaps my only regret is that I will not be there to see it. Let that innate knowledge stir your blood. Risk the unknown. Real wisdom only comes when we drop the pretence of what we think we know and the fears that keep us tame. Understand that nothing is as ordinary as it seems, and there you will find answers and the courage enough to stand for those with no voice."

Annie's words were strong and resonant, as though they came from somewhere else. But then she was done and slumped back in her chair, her eyes closed.

Kayla sat as hours passed, holding the shell spiral snug in her hand, feeling the form and energy of the gift, wondering what else she might find hidden behind this door that had swung so wide.

Later that afternoon Kayla slipped away. How could she possibly ever remember and reconcile all that had happened? It was going to take a while alright. But right now? The only thing she knew for sure was she needed to get to water.

Chappie Cove was the closest. Within minutes Kayla was on the dirt track to the cliff's edge. Below there'd be waves and winds and the fine gravel and minute shells that passed for beach sand around here. Once down on the beach she strode out along the shoreline, till there was nothing but her feet and the abrasive sound of the shells and rocks and the swirling of water as the tide rushed in, filling her footsteps as if she had never been. As it soon would for Annie.

How could she have been given so much, only to have it taken away so soon? Annie's time was nearly over, and with her would pass Kayla's only living ancestral link to her Nan and all that was sacred and magic and inexplicable in the depths of her soul. How could she bear being alone again? Life was precious and fragile and she couldn't stop the tears as they ran down her cheeks and fell into the ocean.

Overhead the gulls followed her along the cove, wheeling and calling till finally grabbing her attention and forcing her back into the outer world. She stopped and looked down the beach, barely able to see the staircase that she'd taken from the cliffside to the shore.

No one was within sight. It was going to be bloody cold, but right now she needed to be held buoyant and close, to taste that sharp bite of salt and feel the tumbling massage of churning water. Kayla stripped and ran into the ocean, diving into water so chilling it took her breath away, and all thoughts except surviving the pull of the tide. Till there was nothing but the moment.

Exhausted, she dragged her pummelled body out onto the sand and lay a while on the waterline as the waves came and went. Nothing would ever stop the momentum of life and the play of time and tides. She lay longer, floating in the to and fro, the push and pull of the shallow waves. Trusting the water even as a maverick wave propelled her firmly onto the shore.

She sat up and shook out a shower of fine shells that had caught in her hair. How was it that she could trust this fierce unpredictable force of nature and yet constantly question everything else? Annie had found such peace and comfort in her unwavering acceptance. Maybe, like those before her, she just had to trust the mystery.

# Chapter 29

Back at the guesthouse, Shirl handed her a letter. Damn it! It could only be bad news. It was too soon and anyway, she wasn't ready. Once back in her room Kayla forced herself to open it. As she dreaded, it was the call back to Australia that she could not refuse. A court case against indiscriminate fracking for shale oil had reached a critical turning point. She had to return within a week to testify. How could she leave this home and family she had only just found?

But there was no choice. After confirming a flight home, Kayla grabbed her bags from the guesthouse and moved into Annie's spare bedroom. There had been unquestionable gratitude in Annie's eyes when she had offered earlier. That night she walked with Annie to her bed and tucked the blankets firmly about her little body, marvelling at the strength of spirit that drives life far beyond mere physical endurance. Kayla sat with her great-great-aunt until she slept. Right now there was nowhere else in whole universe she would rather be.

The next day, at Annie's insistence, Kayla drove back through the craggy hills and down into the port of Hermitage to catch the ferry to Gaultois. Annie had been weaker that morning, as if she had only been hanging on for her. Afraid that she would slip away, it was with great reluctance Kayla had agreed to leave her side even for this day. But if it was important to Annie, it was important to her.

Kayla was determined to put all that aside as she rode the ferry across the fjord to Long Island where her Nan had grown into a young woman. Annie had spoken of distant relations still living in Gaultois, the only outport left on the island itself. Back in the day there had been eight other villages scattered around its shores.

There were only six hours till the last ferry back to Hermitage. She simply didn't have the time or focus to introduce herself properly to any distant kin still living in Gaultois. So, without declaring any family connection, Kayla sought directions to the site of the relocated outport of Piccarie. Annie had given her a mission, and it was all she could think about.

The morning fog had burnt off, leaving a clear sunny day for hiking across the hills. Though stunted by short summers and fierce freezing winters, the woods were lush and thick, ferns and berries and lichens rising from every peat-filled cranny. The rough-trod path took her along the marshy edges of four ponds and up into high barrens where any foliage had been dwarfed by the ravaging winds. Criss-crossing several times, a gurgling brook accompanied her descent as she slithered down into the deserted harbour of Piccarie, its waters sweet and cool and wonderfully refreshing as the day warmed.

Nothing but a scattering of concrete blocks remained where the little village had once stood. As is the way of relocation, the houses had been either demolished or floated intact onto the water to be towed by boat around the coast and brought back to land for settling elsewhere.

Kayla fossicked among the debris for evidence of the people who had striven so hard to sustain life. Many generations of her ancestral line had lived and died here. But there was little to be found. Harsh winters of snow and ice had scoured the cove clean. She climbed the near hill to look out along the rock-strewn shore towards Pushthrough, where Annie said the pirate ship had gone down. Whatever may have remained of the wreck was hidden in the deep dark water below.

But, at last, she was here. Piccarie. The place where her Nan was born, where she had been taught the lore of the sea and the profound love of water that she had sought to pass on to Kayla. Without intention Kayla began humming the melody she had learnt from Annie. It wasn't long before she saw flitting shadows in the water of Hermitage Bay. Not yet ready to take any credit, she was just grateful they were here.

Kayla wandered back down to where the village once stood, thinking, as she walked, of being with Annie on the cliff top. Wisps of the memory danced through her body, physically evoking the same sensual honouring her Nan had encouraged the child, Kayla, to heed.

*Be awake*, her Nan would say as she urged Kayla to hear the water as it spoke, to learn the language of the rocks, depths and shallows of its passage as it gurgled on its merry way. Or the melody in the wind. Or to honour the sacred life of each and every fish they caught and ate together. Kayla closed her eyes to properly feel the tumble of rocks beneath her feet, where home had been for many generations, over several hundred years of ancestral bonding to country.

It was after she'd eaten, as she scanned the small, sheltered inlet, that Kayla saw the seal. Basking on a rock at ocean's edge, its sleek grey fur shining where it caught the light. She crept closer and then closer still. Glistening drops of salty water fell slowly from its leathery hide and back into the sea. Undaunted by her presence, the seal lifted a flipper in a languid wave. It made her laugh out loud. Again the flipper moved, as if beckoning her nearer still. From where she had squatted down, Kayla rose to her full height, moving slowly to come to within a body's length of the rock, into air rich with brine and the pungent tang of wet fur steaming in the warm sun.

The seal's eyes were round, soft and incredibly human. As their gaze met, Kayla's mind filled with the realms of her dreaming. Then as swiftly as it started it was gone, but so too was the seal. With no time for thought Kayla followed, stripping and slipping quickly off the rock's edge down into dark, cold water. At first she lost sight of the seal but then there it was, its shiny head just above the water … watching … waiting … as if for her to follow.

With a slow breaststroke Kayla skimmed across the surface, trailing the seal out towards the rocky entrance of the inlet. Three times the seal dived, returning to the surface further out, enticing Kayla ever onwards. Three times Kayla considered the risks, but the sea was gentle, so, putting her fears behind her, she kicked her heels and followed suit.

Beyond the heads of the harbour, just as they entered the fjord itself, the seal swam off to the left. Waiting just long enough for Kayla to be sure of its position, it disappeared once more below the surface. Patiently treading water, Kayla waited, but the seal seemed to have vanished. Well, this was her element too, so filling her lungs she duck-dived down into the murky depths. Sea-worn boulders lay tumbled along the glacial forged cliffs. It took Kayla several dives before a flicker of movement caught her eye. After returning to the surface for fresh oxygen, she dived down and found herself in an open passage that ran between a series of rocks. She used her hands to pull her body through the crevasse. Her air was nearly gone when she reached the rock at the end. It was a split-second choice to go over or under.

Later she would say that it never was a choice, that she never really considered the top road. Other times she wondered at the price she might have paid. But with a quick flick of her feet she found herself deeper than she'd ever meant to, heading into what could well be a dark, watery grave. But almost at once there was light through the gloom and with a last determined kick, her head broke through the surface into a barely lit cavern. For some minutes she clung to the comforting solidity of the nearest rock and focused on breathing, drawing the thick air deep into starving lungs until her racing heart eased and the spots cleared from her vision.

Kayla pulled her body up out of the water onto a smooth platform of damp rock. Faint light came from above, tinged with green as if filtered through several layers of foliage and moss. Water dripped in an erratic rhythm, in a series of tones determined by the height of its fall. The tang of sea debris was almost overwhelming, yet its pungency strangely reassuring.

It was then that she saw the seal again; the sheen of its fur and the glint of light in the soft tender gaze of its eyes defined its form as separate from the cavern's wall. As if it had waited only to be sure of her recovery, the seal turned tail and disappeared into the shadows.

Though naked, she was not cold. As her eyes adapted, she could see enough to know this was no little cave. The walls were distinguishable by the glimmer of trickling water running down the rock faces. Behind where she had surfaced the light had been consumed by impenetrable darkness, but somewhere further in there was a faint sound of slapping and what could almost have been the murmur of voices.

Kayla came to her feet and made her way deeper in, carefully keeping close contact with the wall at all times. With every step, what had appeared as solid gloom gradually became definable, lit by that indiscernible source of diffused light from above. The muffled sounds got louder, tempting her further in. Wondering at the madness that had brought her this far, Kayla knew she could not turn back now. She was safe enough here in the cavern, and could still swim out whenever she was ready, so long as the weather didn't turn.

The path swung left, with the roof and walls gradually closing in as Kayla entered a side tunnel. But the rock beneath her feet remained smooth, as if polished by aeons of wear. Fairly sure this was the way the seal had gone and the source of the sound and mounting stench, Kayla continued onwards, the growing lightness confirming her choice.

Then there it was, the light at the end of the tunnel. Never before had that cliché been so appropriate. The floor ended at a curtain of water that fell from somewhere above. It camouflaged the entrance, turning the floor into a treacherous downhill slide. Carefully climbing along a cascade of fallen boulders to the side of the steep smooth rock, Kayla made her way out into the light.

Sun streamed in from above, its warmth captured by a natural courtyard no more than ten metres wide. Two massive sentinels of rock, twice that height, separated it from the fjord itself, catching and amplifying the warmth of the sun. A narrow slit, barely half a metre wide, permitted entrance to small wavelets from the ocean beyond.

A family of half a dozen seals basked on a scattering of larger rocks spread across the narrow pebble beach of a small pool. As though acknowledging her presence, the seals began to bark and growl again, in what could pass as conversation. This must be what she had heard sounding like human voices muffled and distorted through the curtain of falling water.

Kayla climbed from the entrance down onto one of the spare rocks. Steam rose from the wet seals, and she sat a while appreciating the comfort of sunlight on her own damp body. She lay back in the hot sun, basking as one of the seal family, long enough to warm her bones through. Through sleepy eyes she scanned the cliff face that enclosed the pool. About two-thirds up there seemed to be a small recess that she just couldn't resist checking out. Chances were, she would never be here again.

The path she found up there was surprisingly easy, as if firmed and established by other feet. By then she was more than ready to move out of the immediate proximity of the seals. No one had ever mentioned how much they reeked. The last couple of metres were the hardest and she had to haul herself up over the edge, but the scrubby tufts of weather-blasted plants she used to pull herself up with seemed as tough as the rocks themselves and might well have been clinging to these cliffs for nearly as long.

It was another cave, though much smaller, perhaps two metres in each direction, and just tall enough for Kayla to stand up in. There was no scent of animal, for which she was grateful. There seemed to be a slight change of colour, and a discernible dip, in the centre of the floor. Crouching down, she ran her fingers across the darkened rock. The fine black dust of a long-ago fire clung to her skin, leaving her no doubt that many fires had been made in the shallow dip, the rock stained by the heat of the burning.

Kayla ran her hands across lichen-lined walls, wanting to imprint the feel, wondering who might have come here and how long ago. And that was how she found them, three distinct markings carved painstakingly into the solid rock. It wasn't that the rest of the wall was smooth, but nature rarely occurs in the distinct straight lines she could feel beneath the living layer. With a loose stone she tentatively scraped back a section of the thin dark lichen that had claimed every surface.

As the pieces peeled away, her adrenaline began to pump, causing a tremble in her fingers. These carvings were the very same symbols carved minutely into the spiral of shell passed down from her great-great-grandmother.

As if in agreement, a cacophony of barking and slapping rose from the seals below. Kayla looked down on their sudden animated performance just as another seal burst through the wall of water, slithering down the smooth rock slide headfirst into the pool without the slightest hesitation, followed by another, and another. It made Kayla laugh out loud, and the cackling joyful spirit of Nunik was all about, leaving her no doubt that this had been her great-great-grandmother's place, her cave, her secret and sacred sanctuary.

She sat for quite some time at the cave's entrance, dangling her legs over the edge, contemplating the miracle of finding this place, let alone being led here by a seal – immensely grateful for the courage given in Annie's words only the day before.

As the sun moved into the afternoon casting long shadows across the rocks, Kayla forced herself to leave. Her only anxiety was the swim out, and that proved considerably easier than coming in. Back in Piccarie Harbour she carefully scrubbed any lingering traces of seal scent from her skin before slipping into the dry layer of clothing she had left onshore.

The hour hike back to Gaultois gave Kayla time to integrate

the experience into the realms where she kept her dreaming and those things she had learnt to keep separate from the ordinary world. But she would never be the same again. Something beyond her own small vision was forcing her to grow, to expand, even if all she knew for now was that she needed to hang on for the ride.

Kayla caught the last ferry from Gaultois back to Hermitage escorted by two different pods of potheads, or jumpers as they were locally known, cresting in exuberant displays between the boat and the setting sun.

Annie was in bed when Kayla crept into the cottage, and she was kind of glad. She barely had the words to begin to share the story of the day, although Annie might just be the only one who would never question the truth of her words.

# Chapter 30

Upon waking, it took a long minute to remember where she was. Kayla's sleep had been a fall into nothingness, a rare treat for one whose nights were often fuller than her days. In the kitchen, Annie was already settled into her favourite chair with a hot pot of strong tea and two cups at the ready, as if quite certain of the moment Kayla would join her.

Annie's welcoming smile dissolved any lingering doubts Kayla still carried about intruding into the older woman's personal space. She took up the second chair, appreciative of the natural silences that seemed as rich and mutual as the conversation that came between them. Beyond the window a storm had moved in from the southwest. The wild weather crossed the bay as the wind and water wove a story of their own dynamic harmony.

After Kayla had cleared away the remnants of a simple breakfast and stoked the wood heater, Annie drew her closer in so she could hold Kayla's hand as they talked. Never one to waste words, Annie's first question was straight to the point. "So tell me what it was you found, my girl."

Kayla told the tale as best she could, trying not to leave out even the smallest detail. In the cold light of a new day it sounded more like a dream than reality, yet across from her Annie hung on every word, often times nodding her encouragement, and other times closing her eyes and breathing in the story as if nourished by the telling.

"And you are sure they were the same symbols there on the wall?" Annie asked, as Kayla concluded.

"Absolutely sure, Auntie. I scraped the black moss or lichen, or whatever it was, back as best I could without damaging anything. Even though it was too dark to see properly, I am in no doubt as to what I felt with my fingers."

Annie clapped her hands in delight. "So it was true then. Well, I'll be darned. Oh, my child, you have just solved a riddle near a hundred years old. There were endless rumours around my mother, being the woman she was. And let me tell you, my girl, she never denied or confirmed a single one, preferring to let the mystery grow and wane as it might. In fact she was known to say no man had ever contained her and no amount of speculation would ever be sure of its own truth. And none ever did."

Kayla just couldn't get enough of the light and pride that animated Annie's face. "I'm kind of amazed she wasn't burnt at the stake in those days," Kayla said.

Annie laughed. "Well, it wasn't quite that long ago. But you are right. It's a good thing that we were a community well steeped in the old ways. As years passed, stories were told over the long nights at winter's hearth, and the name of Mairin began to merge into older myths and tales.

"Remember now, it was Elen who had been washed in from the sea when all others aboard had been drowned. Along this rocky coast that was a miracle of its own. But as for her child, Mairin, well I once heard her described as a wild creature in human form and at the time I did wonder what that made my sister and me. There was a day I became brave enough to ask our mother what they meant but she just smiled in that enigmatic way she had, and said, 'but you already know'."

Annie stopped a moment, slipping into memories long past. "It was said that from an early age Mairin would disappear for hours, or even days on end. Surely it must have been your cave she had found. I've already told you that she could swim like no other, diving into waters that would kill a mere mortal in minutes. And though she might lead the fishermen to a healthy catch, let me tell you that anytime those same men came close to capturing a seal, it would disappear into the deep as if warned of the coming danger.

"And now you are here, young Kayla, with a spirit as wild and courageous as Mairin herself. Telling me how the seals led you to this place." The old woman chuckled and shook her head. "In all my years no other has told of finding this cave. And I have to wonder, even if they had, if any other than yourself would have found the marks of Mairin carved into the stone. If you ever doubted it was in your blood, don't any longer. This is your legacy, child. My question for you is, what do you intend to make of it?"

With this Annie tightened her grip on Kayla's hands, holding her gaze with her own as if peering deep into her soul, seeking answers to the questions Kayla had carried for a lifetime.

"I don't know, Annie. In some ways I feel less certain of anything than I've ever been. And yet, after coming to Newfoundland and being here with you, I feel like I'm teetering on the cusp of something new, and compelling, and it's urging me to shift and grow though I'm not at all sure what that something is. Or that I'm even ready." It sounded weird even as the words tumbled out, but there was truth in it. She just had to push on.

"Nan birthed something deep and different in me, but I've not known how to grow it up. I can stay in and under water longer than anyone. And then there's this empathy with rivers and waterways that is both ecstatic and devastating. As they become more polluted and the heart of the planet sickens, it feels like it's actually happening to me, to my body, and I have to disconnect before … Damn it all Auntie, we are running out of time, and someone must speak out."

"Aye, they must. And you will, of that I have no doubt." Annie nodded. "But I wonder if it is a modern anxiety, this need to know everything and be everything to everyone all at once. It is not so. Watch how nature manages."

"I do. I watch her all the time. But it just seems wrong and foolish to think that humans can be the solution and the great healers when we are the creators of the problems in the first place. Ahggh, it's all so convoluted and mind boggling." Restless, Kayla stood and paced the room.

Annie waited till Kayla's energy settled. "Go to the window now, and look over in the cove where the water is mirror still. It is surrounded by movement and yet, just for this precious reprieve, it is protected from the wind and tides. But do you think for one minute that that water has forgotten all it knows of being a wave? Be certain that when the tide turns, as it does in every life, that that very water will swell and crash upon the shore as if it had never rested. Its inherent nature is present in every mood, every circumstance, able to respond at any time to be whatever it is called upon to be. We come, we go, and in between we must find the peace that will enable us to give what we can."

"But she needs more help than I can give."

"Lucky it's not entirely up to you then."

"But—"

"Oh no, my dear. It's not a superhero or even a battle that's needed. Humans may be changing the face of the earth for all time, and we may yet cause our own demise, but trust her, Kayla.

She cannot resist life in any and all its expressions. She will evolve as she always has, with or without us. For she loves life, without judgement or prejudice. It may never be the same but in the end, life itself will prevail. I trust this beyond all else."

Kayla frowned. "But she's hurting so badly …"

"That she is, maid. That she is." Annie patted the chair. "Come, sit with me again." After a quiet moment of shared sorrow, Annie added, "And that may be so. But it's time to shake the gloom, my girl. You cannot function, drowning in grief. If my own troubled times have taught me anything, it is that hope allows for far more possibility than certainty."

Annie stopped, then reached for Kayla's hand and gave it a sharp tweak, adding, "That, and a willingness to be surprised."

"Ouch!" Kayla flinched. Then Annie laughed out loud, and there it was, in every deep crease of her aunt's face. The same pure mischief lit up the so-familiar eyes such that her Nan was there again, like an underlay, an echo of blood and family that bound her to this woman through all time.

Kayla shook her head. How could she resist the invitation? "You are so like Nan." She laughed. "I don't know how to describe it. It's an irreverence … or a lightness of being, like something I once knew but seem to have forgotten." She stopped suddenly, shocked by the very simplicity of it. "Oh Annie, that's it, isn't it? That this trust … this link … it can break, but it's never broken."

And nor was she. She knew her eyes were shining as she looked up at her aunt. "This is what you wanted, isn't it? That I would understand that this consciousness we have for this briefest of moments is a precious life, even though it might come and go in the time a mountain takes a single breath. Nothing is ever lost." She laughed again. "It's taken me a minute, but I see it now in everything we've shared. We are the echo of the genes and cellular memory of the those who have passed before us, just as profoundly as we will exist in those still to begin the magical miracle of their own dreaming."

Kayla stopped and rocked where she sat, and looked again at her aunt. "I never have been truly alone, have I? Not only that, but there is a little niche in the scheme of all things that is just mine. No matter what." She stopped, and knew her smile was both rueful, and strangely proud. "And that, in itself, makes however much I get to help, or create change, enough?"

Kayla closed her eyes, overcome by an intoxicating wash of love and grief. Whatever she did or didn't do – or fixed, or healed, or just loved, was OK. And that even as she was bound, and held for this mere wisp of time within this corporal body of flesh and bone, she was free. Just like that kite … and the string … and the hand that let it go.

That was all she needed to remember. She had crossed the world seeking the source of this capacity to experience the world through wondrous, joy-filled senses. When Kayla looked again it was still there, that radiant smile of her ageless aunt that linked her to everything, everywhere, for always. This time Kayla basked freely in its warmth.

"I still can't believe I found you."

"But you must. For you are here and no other is more grateful than I." Annie's eyes glistened. "What magic we have made." Annie's voice needed no volume to express the power of her words.

This, Kayla couldn't answer.

"Come here, dear one," was all Annie needed to say. Like a small child, Kayla turned into the open heart of her great-great-aunt. Annie wrapped her thin arms about her and held on as Kayla wept, shedding long pent-up tears of frustration and loneliness. She had needed, beyond any other resource, to come home to this island, and to drink deeply from the well of that very passion, where all that matters and all that nurtures life comes from the very water itself.

# Chapter 31

Annie was slow to rise next day, and even slower to cross the short distance to her chair, leaning heavily on her stick with each step, her tremor worse.

As they shared the quiet of their morning ritual, Kayla found it hard not to keep glancing over at Annie, a rising fear churning in her belly.

Yet, when Annie caught and held Kayla's gaze, there was a strength of will and deep serenity that belied the frailness of the body. As if she had caught and read Kayla's concerns, Annie nodded and smiled with such compassion that Kayla strained to contain the quiver in her lips.

"Have no fear for me, dear Kayla. I have been contemplating this next journey for quite some time now."

Kayla couldn't look up, couldn't show the grief she couldn't hide. She reached for Annie's trembling hand and held it in her own, minutely exploring every ridge and line, the wear of a long lifetime carved in frail skin.

She had no words for all the things she wanted to say. To tell this precious soul how much it had meant to have found her, to spend this time together with family, not only of blood but also of spirit. How it could never be enough. That in the silences and experiences they had shared she had come to know a new kind of peace in her own being, of being seen and recognised in her own right, loved and embraced for the very strangeness in her soul that had brought such loneliness in her youth.

"You know I have to leave tomorrow," Kayla finally said. Strange how there were times when the utterance of such a simple fact could convey so much.

"I know, child."

"And I can't even imagine when I'll get to return."

"I know that, too."

"And it might … might not be soon enough."

"Aye, that may be so. But like the tides, you will return, of that I have no doubt. I'll never be gone from your heart, just from this world as we know it."

*But I'm not ready,* Kayla wanted to howl out loud to whoever it was who could give so much and then take it away so swiftly. "I could change my ticket" was what she said.

"Aye, you could, but where to?"

"To stay …" Kayla began, but looking up, caught the mischievous gleam in Annie's eyes. She couldn't help but smile as Annie nodded.

"Hardest part of living is letting go. There's no cure for it. Soonest we learn nothing is ever truly lost, the freer we are to make the most of what's here. Let's not be wasting time grieving for what's still ahead. How blessed we be that you were guided to my door.

"And dear girl, look what we have done. Together we have sung the wind, and I surely never imagined to be doing that with any other in this lifetime. You have travelled to Gaultois and then on home to Piccarie. No other could have found their way alone to Mairin's cave. My goodness me, what a fine young woman you are. Strong and passionate and full of righteous fight. Stand up and let me look at you."

Kayla stood, slowly at first, shyly squirming like a five-year-old under the gaze of an elder. But then she closed her eyes and, wanting to honour the intent of the request, took a long breath, reaching up into the fullness of her being until she towered over the fading body of her great-great-aunt.

"Yes, my dear." Annie clapped her hands. "There's a spirit in you that would be having the women of our blood singing in their graves. Know that I go to mine assured that the thread is strong. I mean it when I say that none of us who have come before could ever have dreamt of more. But what is clear is that you have much left to do with your years, and I – well, I have my own way to take."

"I just wish I lived closer."

Annie chuckled. "I been thinking that very thought since the day our Mary sailed away to Australia. But then, you would never have been born to become all that you are."

Kayla made a cuppa and another, then a light supper as day passed into night, savouring every precious minute. Often they sat simply holding hands.

Just before she slept that night, Annie pulled Kayla close. "My wish is for you to find trust in those from whom you have come, especially those to whom you belong. Powerful women who stretch back to the beginnings of things, and they all be standing right beside you. There is nothing outside you stronger than that which you already carry inside." As though released of the weight of her words, Annie sighed and closed her eyes.

"You'll always be with me too now, Auntie." Kayla hugged her fiercely, careful not to hold the fine body too tight.

"Yes, maid. That I will." Annie's voice was fading to a whisper.

"Thanks for ... everything."

Annie's answer was a slow smile.

Kayla brought the most comfortable chair in beside Annie's bed.

She barely slept, watching and listening in the thin moonlight to the rhythm of life still present in every breath.

Morning came all too soon. They clung to each other in a final lingering embrace.

Annie pulled back so as to see her one last time, reaching her thin hand to Kayla's cheek, as she had done that first day. "I will almost certainly be gone when you pass back this way, as I am equally certain you will return. And there's no point shaking your head." She laughed. "It is the song of the sea that fills your precious heart, maid. If ever you be needing her strength, go to her shores and call for Nunik, for we are one and the same. Become the 'oneness', as we did together, you and I …" As Annie's voice dropped away, Kayla hugged even tighter.

"But for now, my dear, it's best we be seeing you on your way."

All Kayla could do was drive away. She waved back at the little figure curled over her wooden stick, till Annie merged into the past. The clouds that clung to the hills thickened into rain just as she reached the plateau, forcing her to pull over, the moisture in her eyes blurring her last vision of the fjord known as the Bay d'Espoir.

A couple of hours later, as Kayla turned east onto the Trans-Canada Highway, she couldn't shake the feeling that she was returning from another realm altogether. As if for a time she had slipped through the mists of uncertainty and crossed the thin space that separates the mundane from the lands of magic and myth.